Strudel's Forever Home

Strudel's Forever Home

Martha Freeman

Holiday House / New York

Library of Congress Cataloging-in-Publication Data

Freeman, Martha, 1956–
Strudel's forever home / by Martha Freeman. — First edition.
    pages cm
Summary: "Strudel, a homeless dachshund, loves listening to Jake read from Chief,
Dog of the Old West at the animal shelter. When Jake decides to adopt him, Strudel
vows to be as brave and loyal as Chief. Readers get a dog's eye view as Strudel
narrates this story of a dog who needed a family, and a struggling family who
needed a dog"— Provided by publisher.
    ISBN 978-0-8234-3534-0 (hardcover)
    [1. Dachshunds—Fiction.   2. Dogs—Fiction.   3. Pet adoption—Fiction.
    4. Family life—Fiction.]   I. Title.
    PZ7.F87496Su 2016
    [Fic]—dc23
    2015004330

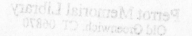

In memory of
my family's dachshund,
Max,
a big dog in
a little-dog body.

Also by Martha Freeman

The Orphan and the Mouse

1,000 Reasons Never to Kiss a Boy

Fourth Grade Weirdo

The Polyester Grandpa

The Trouble with Cats

The Trouble with Babies

The Trouble with Twins

The Year My Parents Ruined My Life

Strudel's Forever Home

One

To look at me, you would never suspect that I was once a shelter dog.

Not to brag, but I am in the prime of life—healthy, good-looking and sleek. I don't have fleas. I don't have bad habits. I can sit up and shake paws. I can roll over with the best of them.

But just over a year ago, a calamity happened in the night. It drove me away from my happy home and human. It drove me out into the street.

For a long time, all I remembered was this: I fell asleep on a soft, familiar pillow, the air around me perfumed by the scent of premium dog food. And I woke up on an unfamiliar doorstep—sniveling and soaked through, every part of me hurting and exhausted, even my tail.

What woke me were gentle but unfamiliar human hands. They lifted me. They brought me indoors. They toweled me off and cleaned me up. After that, another human placed me in a kennel with a bowl of water and a dish of

1

kibble. It was an inferior brand. "Wait! I don't belong here!" I whined.

"That's what they all say," muttered a beagle-cross in a nearby kennel.

The dog in the kennel beside me was kinder. "How are you feeling?"

Her woof was mild, but I jumped as if she'd howled in my ear. "I'm sorry, what? I'm a little shaky."

"Yes, I know," she said. "I heard the humans talking. Are you feeling any better?"

My nice neighbor was a black cockapoo whose smell reminded me of the sugary tea my human sipped before bed. She had bright eyes and a delicate nose. She was elderly and elegant, with a white muzzle and a slight quaver in her voice. Later I would learn her name was Maisie. That morning I knew only that she was sympathetic.

"I feel rotten," I said, "like I've been dunked in a cold river and run over by a bus."

"My, my." The cockapoo looked at me through the wire grid separating our kennels. She was lying down, her head resting on her paws. "And *were* you dunked in a river and run over by a bus?"

"I don't know," I said. "I can't remember a thing."

"Hmm," she murmured. "Perhaps you've suffered some kind of trauma. I think your memory will clear up eventually—if you want it to."

"I just want to go home," I whined. "That is, if I even have a home anymore."

The cockapoo made sympathetic noises. "Do you know where you are now?" she asked.

I didn't, and she explained. I was in the small-to-medium-size-canine room of an animal shelter. The shelter manager, Shira, had found me on the doorstep when she came to work. This was in late August. Maisie herself had been in residence for a month, ever since her own human passed away.

"To put it bluntly, no one wanted me after that," she explained. "I'm like all of us pets here at the shelter, abandoned."

"But I'm not abandoned!" I insisted. "My human loves me!"

"Then he will come for you," said Maisie.

Only he didn't. Days passed, and then a week and then another. Had my human been hurt in the calamity? Hurt . . . or worse? And my happy home, was it gone forever?

Settling into shelter life wasn't easy. There was a continuing rotation of new dogs to get used to, some of them brash and ill-mannered, some of them loud, some of them hardly more than puppies. Every day I expected my human to come, and every day I was disappointed. Through it all, I relied on Maisie to keep my spirits up.

I had been at the shelter about a month when one afternoon Shira brought a boy to meet me.

"I found this fellow on our doorstep one rainy morning," she told him. "He was soaking wet, banged up, no collar."

"You mean he just showed up here?" the boy asked.

Shira nodded. "With dogs, it happens more often than you'd expect. My theory is their super-sensitive noses pick up the smell of food and other dogs inside. So they plop themselves down on the stoop and wait, hoping for a chance to join their new pack."

"Weird," said the boy.

Shira laughed. "Not so weird. Dogs are pretty smart when it comes to survival. Anyway, we haven't been able

3

to find this one's owner. At first he was scared of his own shadow, but now at last he's settling down. I think a little extra TLC—tender loving care—would do him a world of good."

The boy, let's face it, needed grooming. He was skinny, with dark eyes and shaggy black hair. His smell was appealing, though, like earth and tuna fish and packaged cookies. "He's a wiener dog, right?" the boy said. "Does he bite?"

Me? Bite? I have never been so insulted!

"He's a dachshund," said Shira. "And no, he doesn't bite. He seems to have been well brought up."

Thank you, Shira. Yes, I was.

"What's his name?" the boy asked.

Shira said, "We call him Strudel," and I cringed. One of the volunteers had given me that name. Strudel is a German pastry, and I am a German breed. I guess the name was supposed to be funny, but I didn't like it. I wanted something strong and heroic to reflect my true, proud nature.

The boy looked at me doubtfully. "Don't you got a bigger dog?"

"We have dogs of all sizes," said Shira, "but this one needs a friend. Why don't you give him a try? And if you don't get along, you can read to a different dog next week."

Before I knew what was happening, Shira had opened my gate, clipped a leash to my collar and lifted me up, out and onto the white tile floor, which felt cool against my paws.

While the boy listened to instructions, I looked him over. He wasn't wearing socks. His jeans were frayed and his canvas shoes were faded.

"Can I take him now?" the boy asked impatiently.

Shira handed over the leash. "He's all yours."

Oh boy, oh boy, oh boy—I get to go outside!

4

I was so excited I practically dragged the boy down the narrow hallway, and when we got to the sliding glass door I jumped up and pawed the glass.

"Hang on a second, wouldja?" The boy laughed, then yanked the door open. I squeezed out in a hurry.

Ahhh—the smellscape was fantastic. The shelter was built around a small concrete courtyard. The boy and I were the only ones there just then, but all the shelter dogs had visited at one time or another and left their scents behind. There were people smells, too, and regular city ones, like car exhaust and chewing gum and grease.

It was all so delicious under the warm sunshine that I was beside myself. I tugged at the leash, eager to make a thorough investigation, but the boy scooped me up into his arms and sat me down beside him on a metal bench.

Now what? A treat, maybe? I could sure use a treat!

Sadly, a couple of good hard sniffs revealed what I had already suspected: This boy was not carrying dog treats at all. Instead, he had a book in his hand. Seeing it gave me a pang. My human had had plenty of books, a whole library's worth. He was always reading, often while I dozed on a cozy blanket by his side.

I missed my human terribly. I missed everything about that life.

But I wasn't going to think about it anymore. I wasn't even going to think my real name. My memories only gave me a pain behind my eyes—a pain so terrible it made me retreat, whimpering, to a corner of my kennel.

I was through with that now. Maisie might be an old dog, but she was tough, and she had encouraged me. *Summon your hound-dog nature, Strudel,* she told me. *Live in the present.*

"I picked out a special book for us, Strudel," the boy

said now. "It's one my grandpa gave me because he used to read it when he was a kid. It's about a dog, too—only the dog is big and strong, a hero dog. It's an old book from a long time ago, called *Chief, Dog of the Old West*. The author is Thesiger Sheed Lewis."

Chief, Dog of the Old West

After church one Sunday morning, Chief and his family were finishing their breakfast when from out yonder there came an ominous, rattling sound.

Pierre, the French chef, rushed to the window. "Sacre bleu!" he cried. "A rattlesnake has set up housekeeping on the porch!"

Sheriff Silver, the square-jawed family patriarch, made a face. "I hate snakes."

Chief, who was strong and powerfully built, added a comment of his own: Woof.

The widowed sheriff had a brainy, blue-eyed daughter named Rachel Mae who dabbed her lips with her napkin, took up her pencil and said, "I will devise a plan."

Time passed. The rattling grew louder.

At last Rachel Mae proclaimed her plan complete. "The 11th Cavalry under the command of dashing Colonel Joshua Trueheart will stage a flanking maneuver thus." She indicated with her pinkie. "A fleet of warships will steam upriver and anchor in the duck pond. Brandishing traditional weapons, our stalwart Apache allies will advance upon their sturdy mustang ponies."

Chef Pierre looked over Rachel Mae's shoulder and nodded. "This plan reminds me of the Emperor Napoleon's at Waterloo."

Sheriff Silver frowned. "You'll correct me if I'm wrong, Chef Pierre, but I believe the esteemed French emperor lost that one."

"Oui, it's true, and more's the pity," said Chef Pierre. "Had Napoleon won, we here in Groovers Gulch might be speaking French."

"I take your point," the sheriff said, "but as for Rachel Mae's plan, I see a flaw. There is no telegraph in Groovers Gulch, no means to contact either the cavalry, the Navy or our staunch Apache allies."

Rachel Mae did not cotton to being contradicted, and might have made a pert remark . . . except for a raucous disturbance out yonder on the porch.

Unnoticed by his family, Chief had taken matters into his own teeth and paws.

The din was tremendous—rattle-thumpety-rattle-bumpety-snappety-snappety-grrrrr—and after that there fell an eerie silence.

"My puppy! I can't look!" shrieked Rachel Mae.

"Me neither," said Sheriff Silver.

Chef Pierre returned to the window. "The bad news," he reported, "is that the mess is disgusting. The good news is that the snake is now in half a thousand pieces. Once again, the family canine has prevailed!"

"Huzzah!" chorused Rachel Mae and Sheriff Silver. "Long live Chief!"

"I wonder," said Chef Pierre, "in which cookbook I might find a recipe for rattlesnake au vin."

Two

At first, the boy wasn't sure he liked wiener dogs.

But when I turn on the charm, I am irresistible. I rolled over. I played dead. I sat up and begged. I shook paws.

The boy was awestruck. "You know all the tricks, Strudel! I wonder who taught you. It must've been someone who loved you a lot."

My human taught me, and he did love me a lot. But some calamity happened, and now he's gone.

After that, the boy came back and read to me once a week. Over time, I learned all about him. His name was Jake. He was a fifth grader. His teacher had signed him up for this program where kids read aloud to shelter animals. The idea was for the kids to get practice reading while animals got extra attention.

Jake and I both loved the stories about Chief and the Old West. They made me think that I could be a hero, too.

If I had a family of my own the way Chief did, I would save them from rattlesnakes and other mean, rotten varmints. I would protect them from bad guys and outlaws and villains. If I had a family of my own, I would prevail over evil . . . so that peace and justice could triumph.

On a morning in late September, Shira came in and knelt by my crate. "Guess what, Strudel? I have a surprise."

I sniffed, jumped up and wagged my tail: *Oh boy, oh boy, oh boy! Is it liver flavor?*

Shira laughed. "No, Strudel, it's not a treat," she said. "It's better than that. I've just talked to Jake's mom, and this afternoon when he comes, he is taking you away with him. You are getting your forever home at last!"

From the kennel beside me came a sigh that was a cross between a whimper and a moan.

Maisie?

But I was too excited to pay attention. I was going to have a home of my own! Shira left, and I rolled over twice, chased my tail and yipped, then chased my tail and yipped some more.

"Put a lid on it, wouldja?" said TJ, a miniature pinscher who was new to the shelter and grouchy.

"Sorry." I took a breath and tried to settle down, but it was hard. My tail seemed to be wagging itself.

"Strudel's just happy," Maisie said gently. "Wouldn't you be?"

"Happy?" TJ snapped. "I don't expect to be happy again. I'm too old to get used to a new place. And humans don't want old dogs anyway."

"*That* was uncalled for, TJ," said a Chihuahua called Churro, indicating Maisie with his tail.

"Aw, there's no point any of us kiddin' ourselves," TJ snarled. "You gotta be cute, young and friendly to get a forever home. You gotta play the bright-eyed, wag-your-tail, whatever-you-want-boss game that humans always fall for. Then when you do, there're no guarantees they'll be good to you anyway."

"What do you mean?" I asked.

TJ nosed his bedding around and got comfortable. "It's not all chew toys and peanut butter out there. Plenty o' humans forget to take you out, then swat you on the nose when you piddle inside. Then there's humans that'll chain you up in the cold and never let you indoors for a minute."

By this time, my tail was drooping.

I thought Maisie would tell me TJ's stories were just puppy tales intended to scare me.

Only she didn't.

"Who can say what the future holds, Strudel?" she said. "Summon your hound-dog nature, and live in the present. Your new human is only a pup himself, but I'm sure he'll try his best."

Three

Soon after that, Jake was due.

"How do I look?" I asked Maisie.

"Short, long and handsome, Strudel. Same as always," she said. "You are a good-looking young dog."

"Thanks." I sat up on my haunches and tried to "exhibit a noble mien," the way Chief was always doing. Now I could see into Maisie's kennel, and I noticed she still had food in her dish from breakfast. "Are you all right?"

Maisie answered without looking at me. "I'm going to miss you."

"I'll miss you, too," I said, then realized all at once how much I meant it. Maisie's kindness had seen me through the darkest days. She was a sedate old lady and I an energetic teenage pup. Even so, we'd been the best of friends.

What if Maisie didn't get a forever home of her own? New dogs arrived at the shelter all the time. There were only so many kennels. I didn't know exactly what happened to the pets that weren't adopted, but I had heard rumors, and none of them was good.

I wanted to say something hopeful, something to encourage Maisie the way she had encouraged me. But I didn't know what, and before I could get started, the door opened and Shira came in with Jake.

"He knows something's up," Shira was saying. "He's been hyper all day. I hope he settles down at your house, or he won't be very popular with the neighbors."

Were there neighbors? I wondered. What about horses? A French chef? A blue-eyed, brainy daughter?

I couldn't wait to see my new home! I hoped it would be like Chief's—a cottage with a porch under blue skies on the wide, wide prairie.

Maisie said, "Best of luck to you, Strudel. I hope our paths will cross again someday."

I meant to answer, but by this time Jake had unlatched the door to my kennel and I was licking his face. Then Shira clipped the leash to my collar, lifted me out and set me down. I tried to keep calm, but I couldn't. I spun, I jumped, I spun some more. Soon my leash and I were tangled. Churro was laughing, then all the other dogs, too.

"What a ruckus!" said Shira. "Come on outside where we can hear ourselves think."

Jake tucked me under his arm, and just like that, I left the small-to-medium-size-canine room for good.

"Goodbye, everyone!" I howled. "Maisie, I'll miss you!"

"Strudel, quiet *down*!" Jake said. "Mutanski's not gonna like it if you're noisy in the car."

"Moo-tan-skee?" Shira repeated the funny name.

"My mutant teenage sister, Mutanski for short," Jake

said. "People like my mom call her Laura. It's Mutanski that drove me here 'cause my mom's at work."

"Well, that's all right," said Shira. "Your mom and I have already made the arrangements."

By this time we were standing on the sidewalk outside the shelter. I hadn't been there since the awful day I arrived, and a strange feeling came over me. The sky went dark. I felt exhausted and scared and sore. I began to tremble and cower.

Wise Maisie had told me about something called a flashback. It meant you remembered something so powerfully you lived it over again. Was I reliving the calamity? If I was, the view was in bits and pieces—rain, flashing lights, rough pavement against my paws.

"Strudel?" Jake said. "Hey, Strudel, what's the matter, buddy?"

"Oh dear," said Shira. "This used to happen to him sometimes when he first got to the shelter. Something bad must've happened before he came to us. Hey, boy? You okay?"

Jake's and Shira's voices seemed to come from far away. Gradually I became aware of Jake's arms and ribs, of Shira's fingers scratching me behind the ears. When I looked around, it was light—daytime. I didn't hurt anymore. Everything was fine.

Shira said, "I think he's coming around. Change can be unsettling for a dog, or for anyone. If there's any trouble, you feel free to call us."

Jake nodded. "Okay."

A girl came up to us. She smelled like the greasy egg rolls she ate for lunch, as well as many polishes and lotions. She had paper-white skin, red lips and straight black hair.

"You must be Jake's sister," Shira greeted her.

"Mutanski," Jake said.

The girl frowned. "I'm *Laura*," she said to Shira. "Nice to meet you."

Jake's sister was nothing like Rachel Mae. Instead of lace and ribbons, she wore shorts, boots and a torn T-shirt. Her eyes were brown, not blue. Was she brainy? Hard to tell.

Shira wrapped me and Jake in a big hug and told us to take care of each other. There was a tear in her eye, and she wiped it with the back of her hand. "I've got to get back to work," she said.

Mutanski pointed to a car parked at the curb. I don't know much about cars, but I could see this one was old. There was a dent in the door, and the paint was coming off in patches.

"Backseat, you two," Mutanski said.

Oh boy, oh boy, oh boy—car ride! I just love car rides!

And this car—wow! Did it ever smell delicious! Sweaty socks, spilled soda, the stale remains of greasy human snacks. *Yummy!*

I thought of my previous human's car, which had smelled disgusting—almost as bad as the worst of all possible things, shampoo.

"You'll be fine, won't you, Strudel?" Jake pulled me close. "I bet you like car rides."

I sure do!

"Strudel?" Mutanski started the motor. "You can't be serious. Is that his name?"

"It's his shelter name till I think of something else," Jake said, "something brave-sounding. I know he's small, but in his heart he's a hero."

Got that right!

Mutanski, meanwhile, was laughing like she'd never heard a better joke.

"Shut up!" Jake defended me.

"Don't tell me to shut up. I am doing you a favor by driving you at all," said Mutanski.

As the car pulled into traffic, I tried *really really hard* to be still, but I'd been cooped up a long time, and this was so exciting!

How could I resist dashing from window to window?

How could I help but greet the dogs I saw, and all the other creatures, too—creatures unlucky enough not to have been born dogs? On the streets outside the window now were horses pulling carriages. We must be in the Old West for sure!

"Sheesh, Jake, what is your mutt doing?" Mutanski shouted over my joyful barking. "Can't you make him lie down?"

"Strudel—*quiet!*" Jake pulled me back into his lap. "Now let's look out the window, okay? This neighborhood is called Old City. See the brick buildings? They're hundreds of years old. That one is where the Declaration of Independence was signed. Our class took a field trip last year."

"Oh great, teach your *dog* American history," said Mutanski.

"You're just embarrassed because he already knows more than you," said Jake.

Mutanski's answer was a snort. The car stopped and started again. It turned left, then right onto a wide boulevard. There were no more horses outside, just cars and people walking.

"If you're so smart," Mutanski asked her brother, "what's that building there?"

"Uhhh . . . ," said Jake.

"Ha!" said Mutanski. "It's Old Swede's Church, and it's older even than Independence Hall. Some of the first Europeans to live in Philadelphia built it."

"There were Swedish people in Philadelphia?" Jake said. "I thought only Italians, like Grandpa."

"Swedes and Germans and Irish in this neighborhood—people from all over," said Mutanski. "You're not the only one who takes history in school."

I looked out the window and saw a low building behind a long brick wall. It didn't look special . . . except for one thing. It was familiar. Had I seen it before? Had I been here with my previous human? I couldn't tell unless I smelled it; I couldn't smell it from the car.

But the sight bothered me. When my human hadn't come to get me at the shelter, I concluded he was gone and with him my home and everything else in my old life, too. Now here was something familiar. Was it possible I had been wrong?

There was no time to think more about it then, though. The car turned right onto another big boulevard, then left onto a narrower street.

"This is our neighborhood, Strudel. It's called Pennsport," Jake said. "And now we're going down 2 Street. Every year around New Year's, they have a big crazy party here. My grandpa is part of it—he's what you call a Mummer. Have you ever heard of Mummers?"

Mutanski snorted again. "Give it a rest, Jake. Your dog doesn't care about American history, or Mummers either!"

"How do you know?" Jake asked. "He likes stories, don't you, Strudel?"

I do! I do! I do!

There were two more turns onto narrow streets before

Mutanski twisted the steering wheel, backed up, twisted the steering wheel again. Finally we came to a stop.

"We're here, buddy!" Jake opened the door and set me down on the sidewalk. "We had to park a couple blocks from home, but you like to walk, right? You're a dog."

Four

My first sniffs of my new neighborhood were not what I expected. I can't claim I know exactly what a prairie smells like, but I was pretty sure it wasn't this: well-fed pets, urban wildlife, greasy fast-food waste, flies and other bugs, gobs of sweet, chewed-up chewing gum flattened on the sidewalk.

As for the sounds: sirens, a basketball slapping asphalt, car horns and human voices yelling.

Where was the call of the whippoorwills?

So much for wide-open spaces.

I reminded myself that Jake had never actually said his home place was like Chief's. I had imagined that part myself. I decided to follow Maisie's advice: I would live in the present, not the past—and that meant getting busy and learning all I could about my new neighborhood. A dog gets information through his nose, so as Jake and I walked, I stopped at every bush, tree, post and corner.

Unlike my previous human, Jake was not used to walking a dog. Soon he became impatient and tugged the leash. "Come on, Stru. Let's go! We haven't got all day, you know."

Mutanski looked back over her shoulder. "Already complaining? I *knew* you weren't responsible enough to have a dog."

After that, Jake let me stop whenever I wanted. Soon I learned that my closest canine neighbors were both males, one a poodle and the other a Staffordshire terrier, which is the breed more commonly called a pit bull.

Both these dogs were big, a lot bigger than me. The poodle was about my own age and the terrier much younger, hardly more than a puppy. There was more information in their scents, too. The poodle was an independent type, not part of anyone's pack, while the pit bull was timid, maybe even a coward. If I had to guess, I'd say he was bullied by his littermates.

I was checking out a fresh marker from the poodle when Jake tugged at me again. "This is it, Strudel," he said, "your brand-new home. My mom's at work, but she'll be here for dinner."

I had been replying to the scent the poodle had left on the dirt surrounding a spindly tree at the curb. Now I turned around and looked at my new place.

It was not a cottage with a front porch on the lone prairie. It was what's called a row house—brick, three stories high, no space between it and the houses to the right and left. Two concrete steps led to the stoop and then a black front door. Mutanski had left the door ajar. I followed Jake up the steps, which were tall for a dog of my stature, crossed the threshold and inhaled.

The human odors were powerful. There were Jake's

and Mutanski's, of course, a third that must represent their mother . . . and a fourth human, too, an adult male.

I can't tell as much about humans from their scents as I can about dogs, but this last one was stale and unpleasant. Right away, I thought of the bad guys in the Chief stories and the humans TJ had warned me about.

My preliminary sniffing done, I looked around. In front of me to the left I saw a stairway, which I later learned led to the bedrooms on the second floor. In back was the kitchen, with a set of sliding doors that went out to a tiny patio. Ahead to my right was the living room.

And all of it was a mess!

I couldn't help but think of the Chief stories. In them, Pierre the French chef is also maid, butler and stable hand. Rachel Mae says every well-run household needs a Pierre.

So where was Pierre now?

Sweaters, hoodies, shoes, water bottles, socks, magazines, books, papers, pens, pencils, coats and umbrellas lay wherever they had happened to fall—on the floor, the chairs, the tables or the sofa.

I like messiness as much as the next dog, but I wasn't used to it. My early memories are of a clean bed of excelsior and my mother's warm body and good milk, the snug feeling and familiar smells of my littermates. From there I had gone to live with my previous human, who had tidy habits and a house-cleaner once a week.

In Jake's house, things were obviously going to be different.

"Whaddaya think, Strudel?" Jake unclipped my leash and set it on top of a pile of loose shoes by the door. "It's not beautiful, I guess, and it's not the Old West like where Chief lives. But it's home, and we'll treat you good."

Jake's kind voice reassured me, and I rolled over for a

tummy rub—*awww*. Maybe the fourth human I had smelled would never come back. Maybe I'd get used to messiness. Anyway, there were lots of tastes and smells and textures to investigate.

"Come on and I'll show you upstairs," Jake said. It took him only a second to sprint to the top, but I looked up in dismay. A dachshund's short legs are meant for digging, not climbing stairs.

Jake looked back and saw the trouble. "Oh, Stru, I didn't think of that. I guess I'll have to carry you till you're used to 'em."

At the top, Jake's room was on the right, Mutanski's (its door shut tight) on the left. Down the hall, their mom's looked out on the front sidewalk.

None of the bedrooms was big compared to the rooms in my old home, but they were all a lot bigger than my kennel at the shelter. I wagged and woofed to tell Jake I approved.

"Do you want to play, Strudel? Is that it?" Jake asked.

Sure! Playing is good! I always want to play!

Jake tore a piece of paper from a notebook, wadded it into a ball and threw it . . . right under the bed. The floor was wood, no carpeting, and my toenails clicked as I chased it into a maze of abandoned objects, a fog of dust and cobwebs. The objects—paper plates, candy wrappers, a Pringles can—were all very interesting, but I had gone in to get that paper and I would come out with it.

We hound dogs are relentless that way. We can't help it.

Finally I emerged with the paper between my teeth. Jake laughed. "You're covered in crud, buddy." He wiped my eyes and nose bare-handed.

I dropped the paper, accepted a scratch behind my ears and prepared to fetch again. But before Jake could even throw, I heard the front door open and footsteps . . . heavy footsteps.

Oh no! Oh no! Danger! A lily-livered polecat is afoot— one that'll hog-tie us all and steal the meat right out of the fridge!

Five

I spun and barked till Jake said, "Shut up, Strudel!"

Then I spun and barked some more.

Now Jake was pleading. "You'll get us both in trouble, Strudel. I don't think Mom has had a chance to tell him yet."

Tell who what? You mean Mom talks to meat thieves?

"Hey! What's the racket up there? What is that, a *dog?*" asked the thief.

Jake shook his head and closed his eyes. "The man's a genius."

Now the heavy footsteps approached on the stairs. Jake grabbed me, dropped down on the bed and pulled me close. I smelled cigarette smoke, motor oil and aftershave lotion. Then a big man with gray-brown hair appeared in the doorway. He was wearing a green shirt with a picture of a mean-looking bird on it.

"*Jee*-hoshaphat!" The man locked eyes with me and shook his shaggy head. "I hope to glory you ain't planning to *keep* that mutt. Your mama's got better things to do with her money."

The man's booming voice reminded me of the noise on the night of the calamity. If ever there was a thieving, lily-livered polecat, this guy had to be it.

"Small dogs don't eat much, and he's mine, not Mom's." Jake did his best to sound brave, but I could feel his heart, and it was beating fast.

I let loose a rumbling growl.

"And keep him away from me, too, you hear?" the man continued.

"Are you afraid of him?" Jake asked.

"Of that thing? He's hardly a dog at all, more like a weasel."

A weasel, huh? I'll show you!

With a mighty wiggle, I freed myself, jumped to the floor and made like a torpedo toward my target, the big man's right sneaker.

"Strudel—*no!* Leave Arnie alone!"

Leave Arnie alone? Are you kidding? And miss an opportunity for peace and justice to triumph?

With one snap of my powerful jaws, I latched onto the shoe and didn't let go.

But now I had a new problem. Having caught him, what to do with him? Sheriff Silver would have frog-marched this outlaw to jail. Jake's family probably didn't even have a jail.

Kicking and squealing, my captive leaned over and reached for something—a book from Jake's shelf, a book to use as a weapon on me!

I cringed, anticipating the blow, but the dirty rotten varmint was so clumsy he missed, tripped over himself and almost fell to the floor.

This gave Jake time to yank me free of the shoe, which wrenched my jaw—*ow!*

At least no books would be hitting my head.

"He bit me!" cried the lily-livered polecat. "I bet there're tooth marks dug into my flesh! I bet I'm bleeding!"

Jake said, "Look, Arnie, I'm sorry. He just got here, and he doesn't know what's what. You're sorry, too, aren't you, Strudel?"

With his thumb, Jake pushed my chin up so I looked him in the face. If he expected to read apology in my big brown eyes, he had another thing coming: *Let me down! Please let me down! I want to bite him again!*

I'm pretty sure Jake understood, but he played dumb. "See?" he told Arnie. "You can tell he's sorry."

Meanwhile, the outlaw sat down on the edge of Jake's bed and tugged off his right shoe—creating a stink cloud that filled the room.

Bleah!

It's true we dogs get it wrong sometimes about who's a bad guy. We've been known to growl at letter carriers, police officers and even Girl Scouts. But we dogs don't get it wrong for long. And no good guy ever had a foot that smelled that bad.

Six

I didn't bark at Jake's mom when she came home. Her scent reminded me of Shira's, only with a bit more scouring powder (*bleah!*) in the mix. She greeted me by patting my head, but she seemed distracted. I rolled over twice, spun around and wagged my tail.

Hi! Hi! Hi! Hi! Hi! I'm your new dog! I'm so glad to be here! Hi! Hi! HI! Hi! Hi!

"He likes you, Mom! See?" Jake said.

"Unh-*hunh*." Her smile was tired—too tired for enthusiasm, either for a new dog or for anything else. "Could somebody set the table, please? Any back talk and you're toast."

"Aye, aye, Mom," said Mutanski, whose lipstick was now pale purple.

Arnie—aka Mr. Stinky Foot—was still around, sitting at the table in the kitchen drinking beer from a can. My previous human used to drink beer sometimes. But he always put his in a glass. "What's the matter, sugar?" Arnie asked Jake's mom.

"Exhausting day," she said. "It's tough cleaning house. You should try it and see."

"But you're the manager," said Arnie. "I thought you sat behind a desk all day with your feet up."

"Very funny," said Mom. "I don't do that on the best days, and this wasn't one of those. Amber was out sick. I had to do her work *and* mine."

"Aww, sugar. Take a load off, why don't ya? Want a beer?"

Mom took a head of lettuce and some carrots from the fridge. "I need to get some vegetables into these kids," she said. "Their grandpa's bringing pizza in a few."

"The kids' grandpa?" Arnie frowned. "You mean your father's coming over?"

"It's Friday night," she said. "He always brings pizza on Friday night."

Arnie sighed. "Guess I forgot."

"Try not to fight with him," Mom said, "for once?"

Arnie did not reply to that.

I heard all this from a spot beneath the table. Jake and I had followed Mom into the kitchen. He began to retrieve plates from the cupboard. By this time, I was getting mighty hungry. Any second, someone was going to feed me, right? But when I looked around for a dog dish, I didn't see one.

At my previous home, my dish had been made of white pottery, with a picture of a handsome dachshund on the side. My human had washed it twice a day, even though this was unnecessary. Being an excellent eater, I invariably licked it clean.

All of a sudden, my hunger pangs were joined by pangs of sadness. Even though my loyalty was to Jake now, even though I wanted to do what Maisie said and look forward, I could not forget my previous human.

Come to think of it, he was like Maisie in some ways, elderly and quiet. He was not the kind of human you played Frisbee with. He never would have balled up a piece of paper and thrown it under the bed for me to fetch. But he had been kind and gentle.

And he had never once forgotten to feed me right on time.

When Grandpa arrived, I barked two neat little barks to announce his presence, not to sound an alarm or scare him away. He was carrying a pizza, and no black-hearted, lily-livered polecat ever showed up carrying pizza.

Maybe it was because I'd been thinking about my previous human that Grandpa's smell reminded me of his— shaving cream, well-worn clothes and dust. Grandpa walked with a stoop. His face was wrinkled like a bulldog's. On his head his gray hair was so sparse that pink scalp shone through here and there. I wondered if maybe he had a mild case of mange.

"*Grandpa!*" Jake greeted him with a hug. "Look at what I got—my own dog! Isn't he great?"

"Sainted Maria!" Grandpa shook his head. "Is that a dog or a *hot* dog?"

Frowning, Jake took the pizza box. "You are not funny, Grandpa."

I agreed with Jake. At the same time, I would have forgiven this guy anything in exchange for even a tiny morsel of the sausage I could smell on the pizza. Heck, I would have forgiven him in exchange for a greasy corner of the cardboard box.

Had they brought me here to starve, or what? I was getting really worried. Mutanski came in. The family sat down to eat. I had a hopeful thought. Maybe this was one of those households where the dog eats people-food from the table. I knew from some of the small-to-medium-size canines that this kind of paradise existed. My previous human gave me cookies sometimes, but never from the table. He would have found that idea disgusting.

The family talked as they ate. One topic was the game called football, especially the team called the Eagles. It turned out the bird on Arnie's shirt was one of these eagles. My previous human did not care for football, so I had missed out on the pretzels and snacks my dog buddies told me were easy pickings when games were on TV.

From what they were saying, Jake and his family loved the Eagles. Maybe there would be a game tonight. Maybe I would be dining on nachos and onion dip.

The thought made me so hungry, I almost missed it when the humans started to talk about me.

"Dogs are a lot of work," Grandpa was saying, "and who's going to take care of him when you go away?"

Mutanski laughed. "When is it we ever go away?"

"And if we ever did, you could watch him, Grandpa," Jake said.

"I would be embarrassed to be seen with a dog like that," said Grandpa.

"Those were my words exactly," said Arnie.

"Were they?" said Grandpa. "Then maybe I should reconsider."

"*Dad?*" Mom said.

"Aw, he's just a kidder," said Arnie. "Right, Mr. Allegro?"

Grandpa didn't answer. Instead, he pushed his chair back and regarded me where I lay beside Jake. I did what I could to make myself adorable, but it was hard work. I was beginning to get wobbly. So far the only thing that had fallen my way was a lettuce leaf, and a lettuce leaf is not sustaining.

"What time did you feed Killer, here?" Grandpa asked. "He looks peaked."

"Jake?" his mom said.

"Feed him?" Jake repeated. "Oh gosh—I didn't! I guess I figured he ate at the shelter."

"You need to eat more than once a day, and so does he," said Mom. "He must be starving."

I am! I am! I am!

"I told you he wasn't responsible enough to have a dog," said Mutanski.

Jake stood up. "Where's his food, Mom?"

Yesss! My mouth watered, and I would've spun around and wagged my tail—except I was too weak.

Mom's face fell. "Uh-oh. My turn to be embarrassed. The pet aisle is not on my usual grocery route. I completely forgot to buy dog food."

Mutanski snorted and rolled her eyes. "I should've known. Mom's not responsible enough for a dog either."

"Oh, pipe down," said Mom. "I'll pick up dog food tomorrow when I'm out. As for tonight, we can just make do. There has to be something around here a dog can eat."

"I don't think pizza's good for him," Jake said.

Yes, it is! I jumped up and put my paws on his chair. *Trust me! Pizza is good for dogs! Good, good, good!*

"Well, I hope you don't expect *me* to share," said Arnie, and he took the last piece from the box.

Seven

My first dinner in my new home was not prepared by Chef Pierre. It was not premium dog food. It was not even cheap kibble like they served at the shelter. My first dinner in my new home was Lucky Charms cereal. It is sweet and crunchy, all right, but it doesn't fill you up the way dog food does. And those tasty little marshmallows get stuck in your teeth.

I ate three bowlfuls.

But my hound-dog digestion was never built for so many artificial colors and flavors. In the middle of the night my tummy woke me and, in a hurry, I leaped from Jake's bed.

It could have been worse. The multicolor mess landed on the rug, not the pillowcase. And Jake slept through the whole disgusting episode. In the morning, his cry, *"Ewww,* Strudel! *Gross!"* woke me up.

I was truly sorry. On the other hand, who was it that fed me three bowls of Lucky Charms?

Mom heard Jake and came running. "Oh, for the love of

Mike," she said when she saw the rainbow display. "Jake, there're rags in the bathroom and spray cleaner under the sink. Take care of that before school, or so help me, he's going back to the shelter! I don't have bandwidth for one more thing, kiddo, I am telling you."

I thought of what TJ had said about some humans. Was Mom one of them? Would I get swatted on the nose for something I couldn't help?

Maybe I should run away—back to the shelter. Shira and the volunteers had a lot of animals to take care of, so it wasn't like having a family of your own. But at least the meals were on time . . . and Maisie was there.

"I'll clean it up, Mom. I promise," Jake said. "The cereal must have upset his stomach."

"Well, that's just great," said Mom. "So what do we feed him this morning?"

"Maybe we can borrow real dog food from Lisa's family," Jake said.

Real dog food! Yeah! Good idea! Good idea! Who's Lisa?

Mom said, "That's a possibility. I'll send Laura over to ask. And one more thing. Put the beast out on the patio when you go to school."

"Sure. Absolutely. Okay." Jake was being extra obedient so Mom would calm down. We dogs know that routine by heart.

While Jake cleaned up, he told me Lisa was a girl in his class at school, and she lived with her family across the street.

"Her poodle's name is Rudy," Jake said. "I'll take you to the dog park, and you'll probably see him. He goes all the time. Lisa says he has a ton of energy he has to burn off."

Rudy, huh? I had liked his scent, and it was good to put a name to it. With luck, I'd soon be meeting him nose-to-nose.

Mutanski grumbled about going out, but came back with two scoops of dog food and even scratched my back when no one was looking. The kibble was top of the line, too. This Rudy fellow must have a cushy deal.

I ate a bowlful, and for the first time in a while my belly felt comfortable. This cheered me up so much I didn't even mind when Jake set me down on the patio and said, "G'bye, Strudel. I hope you're okay out here. Try not to bark and bother Mrs. Rodino next door. She's a cat person, and grumpy because her last one just died. I'll be home from school around 3:15, and then we'll play."

Play! Yes! Absolutely! Playing is good, good, good!

I gave him my best big-eyed, adorable expression. Then the door slid closed, and through the glass I watched him walk away. Now I was alone, and I wanted to howl with longing. My human would be gone for hours! I hoped he wouldn't forget me.

Eight

Dachs means "badger" in German, and a dachshund is a badger hound—bred to chase badgers for the humans who want to hunt them. Since badgers dig burrows underground, we dachshunds were bred to be low to the ground and diggers, too.

In stories, the badger characters are usually shy and humble. In real life, they are mean, nasty and ferocious. We dachshunds, being smaller than they are, have to be smarter—and braver, too. When necessary, we will ignore fear and pain to get the job done.

That is just the way we dachshunds roll.

Now I used the skills of my breed to check out the patio, my new domain. It was small, maybe half the size of the kitchen. Its floor was made of paving stones, which felt cool and damp to my paws. There was a picnic table with attached benches in the middle, and a barbecue in the corner. Here and there were potted plants, some healthier than others.

Two sides of the patio were enclosed by the brick walls of the houses next door. The wall of Mrs. Rodino's house extended about three-quarters of the way to the alley. The rest of that border was a solid wooden gate. The patio's back boundary was an ivy-covered fence. In front of it was a boxwood hedge.

To make the space homey for me, Jake had set out a mixing bowl full of water and a cereal bowl with the last of Rudy's kibble from breakfast. For a bed, he'd given me a worn pink pillow that smelled good, like Mutanski.

Inch by inch and scent by scent, I gathered information about this new territory. I was investigating a sharp, sour smell in a corner beneath the hedge when I got a snoutful of creepy crawlies—*ewww! Ants!*

I wouldn't nose around *that* corner again.

Elsewhere, I smelled beetles and roaches, stray bits of old food, lighter fluid and charcoal (sickening), old cooked meat (yummy), plastic gardening pots, muddy trowels, a hoe and canvas gloves.

The odors told me there was a rat living somewhere nearby, but this I could tolerate. Rodents are everywhere, and unless this one made himself annoying to me or my humans, I could safely ignore him.

I also picked up the subtle background odor of—forgive me, but there's no way to say this politely—*cat*. Sadly, few places are free of this foul stench. At least the odor was old. No cat had actually entered the territory for a long time, and if I had my way, no cat would.

My investigation almost complete, I had begun to think about a nap on my pillow when, in the corner by the screen door, I saw something coiled, green and menacing. . . .

My ears pricked, my tail straightened and my heart jumped into my throat.

I had never seen such a thing in real life, but I recognized it right away from the first Chief story Jake ever read to me.

It was a rattlesnake!

True, this particular one smelled like rubber rather than flesh and blood—but its fiendish cleverness couldn't fool me. That rubbery aroma must come from the lethal poison in its fangs.

Setting myself firmly on all four paws, I waited. Soon it would give itself away with its rattle. Wasn't that what the one on Chief's porch had done?

But this fellow turned out to be extra sneaky. No matter how patiently I waited, he kept still and silent. Finally, I couldn't stand the suspense. I leaned back onto my haunches. I prepared to pounce. I growled . . . and even then the snake did not so much as blink!

I concluded it must be asleep.

And I couldn't attack a sleeping creature. Only barbarians do that. So I barked to awaken it; then, for good measure, I barked some more.

From the house on the left, I heard scraping. I looked up and saw a woman leaning out of an open window above me.

"Hey, you down there, quiet! You hear me?"

Uh-oh. This must be Mrs. Rodino. But no fair! If she could yip at me, I ought to be able to yip back.

And I did, too, but only a little. I had more important things to worry about—like deadly serpents in my own backyard.

Mrs. Rodino yelled, "I'm warning you, dog!" Then she closed the window.

Guess I showed her!

My eyes returned to the snake, which still hadn't

blinked. At least I didn't think it had. Do snakes have eyelids? For that matter, where was its head?

Oh, to heck with being civilized. It was time to put this venomous monster out of its misery and . . . *attack!*

With a last warning snarl, I sprang forward and snapped my jaws, neatly puncturing the creature's flesh, which tasted—*yum*—like a brand-new chew toy. As for the blood, it was as clear as water.

Soon the snake's green flesh was shredded, and I could step back, survey the carnage and enjoy my victory.

Wouldn't Jake, Mutanski and Mom be grateful? Just like Chief, I had prevailed over evil so that peace and justice could triumph.

Nine

It wasn't Jake but Mutanski who let me back inside that afternoon. Earlier, she had left the house with pink lips. Now they were painted pale blue.

Not that I cared. I was just *happy, happy, happy* that one of the humans was home!

I rolled over, spun in circles, sniffed her shoes and licked her hands. Where had she been? Did she also go to that place called school? She tasted like potato chips, ink and strangers—besides the usual lotions and sprays. When she bent down and gave me a hug, her breath smelled like mayonnaise. I tried to get a taste, but she pushed me away.

"*Bleahh*—Strudel! No doggie kisses! Yes, you're a good dog, you are, and I'm glad you're glad to see me. Look at that tail wagging!"

It's true that when I'm happy my tail takes on a life of its own. "Okay, enough now," said Mutanski. Then she stood, went over to the fridge and opened the door.

Anything in there for me?

Rudy's food had been gone for hours. Hoping to get Mutanski's attention again, I chased my tail, which is funny every time to a human. Then, to mix it up, I lay down and rolled over.

"Hey—cute!" said Mutanski. "I didn't know you could do that! How about a cookie?"

Cookie! Cookie! Cookie! Yes!

I opened my mouth and let my tongue loll. Mutanski went to the cupboard and opened a blue package. The sugar and fat smelled delicious. Chocolate? *Yuck.* But I could overlook it just this once, and almost before I knew the cookie was in my mouth, I had swallowed it.

Eating fast is a bad habit of mine.

To earn a second cookie, I repeated my tricks: roll over, shake, sit up, beg . . . I threw in one more tail chase, even though I was getting dizzy.

"Super cute, Strudel, but no more cookies," Mutanski said. "We can't chance another barfing incident. Anyway, you're supposed to be Jake's dog. Mom's idea is that taking care of you will teach him responsibility, which is sort of a laugh coming from Mom."

I get it—no more cookies! But how 'bout a little bologna?

If Mutanski understood this, she didn't let on. A second later I heard footsteps on the front stoop, then the click and bump of the door latch. Wasting no time, I ran to the living room and sat down, ready to sing a loud, long song of welcome.

My human's home! My human's home—yippee!

Jake didn't mind a bit when I licked his face.

What was this place called school, anyway? Obviously there were lots of other kids there. I could smell them. I

39

could also smell his teacher—hairspray, coffee and breath mints. I remembered because once she had come to the shelter with Jake to visit.

"Thanks for letting him in," Jake said to Mutanski.

She shrugged. "He was pretty excited when he heard someone was home."

"Did you give him water?" Jake asked.

"Hey, he's not *my* responsibility. I don't even like dogs. Now you gotta take him for a walk, remember?" Mutanski said.

"I'll do it later," Jake said, "after I play some *Random Apocalypse*. He's been outside all day, y'know."

"Outside is not the same as a walk. He needs to, uh . . . do his business. Plus he needs exercise."

"Oh, all right." Jake shook his head. "Sheesh, you're as big a nag as Mom."

Oh boy, oh boy, oh boy—a walk!

I dashed to the front door and sat down beside the pile of shoes there.

"Whoa, *good dog*! See that, Mutanski? It's like he knows what we're talking about," said Jake. "He is really smart."

"He's got to be smarter than he looks," Mutanski said.

But she didn't mean it. I was beginning to get the idea about Mutanski. Most of the bad stuff she said she didn't mean, especially when she was talking to her brother.

Jake pushed the door open, and the second he did I rocketed outside and down the steps, tugging my human along behind me.

Ten

My walk the day before had been brief, so this was my first real chance to explore the neighborhood. Red and orange leaves were scattered everywhere on the sidewalk—pretty, but uninteresting smell-wise. Much better was the litter: flattened plastic drink bottles, chip bags, used tissues, candy wrappers and dirty paper plates.

It was like an all-you-can-sniff buffet!

But Jake would not let me at it. I pulled this way, he pulled that. Sometimes it's one big frustration, being a dog.

On the corner was a power pole very popular with dogs, and there I stood my ground. This was obviously canine message central, and there were tons of replies to the message I had left yesterday. Typical was one from the poodle, Rudy. Roughly translated, it said: "Welcome to the neighborhood, dachsie! Sniff you soon!"

Only a few were unfriendly: "I hope you're not as conceited as the last dachshund we had around here." That came from a Pekingese, which I thought was pretty funny. Everyone knows how stuck-up *they* are.

Two of the messages were puzzling—both the same, both warnings: "New dog, whatever you do, keep away from the Pier 67 Gang."

This did not sound good, but what did it mean? Who or what was the Pier 67 Gang?

The very name sounded scary—criminal, almost. I shuddered and for some reason remembered the night of the calamity. Next thing I knew, the strange feeling came over me again. The day seemed to turn dark, the air felt cold and clammy. Was I hearing explosions? Against my will, I began to tremble.

"Strudel?" Jake had been playing with his phone, but now he knelt next to me. "Did somethin' scare you, buddy? You're okay." He ran his hand down my long dachshund spine. "Everything is fine."

I shook myself. What was I afraid of, anyway? My human was here, wasn't he? The daylight came back, and the sun shone. Pier 67 Gang, indeed. Whatever that was, it wouldn't bother *me*.

I lifted my leg to acknowledge messages received. That way when dogs met me nose-to-nose they would be ready to include me in the neighborhood pack. Speaking of which, here came that pit bull, the shy one who must live nearby. He was walking on a leather leash with a male human. Like Jake, this human was a kid, but bigger and older.

The pit bull was twice my size and looked tough—except for his goofy smile. I raised my nose and tail, puffed out my chest and strode toward him. He might be the big dog, but I was the boss—a fact I planned to establish right away.

Watching me approach, the pit bull dipped his snout

respectfully. I figured I'd head butt his leg—*Hey, wanna wrestle?*—but Jake pulled me back.

Meanwhile, the pit bull's human was talking. "Little Jakey Allegro," he said, "how ya doin'? And what's that—a salami you're walking? You better keep him away from Luca here. He might think you're offering up a snack."

"Hi, Anthony." Jake's voice was low. Was he afraid of this Anthony fellow? Did Jake need protection? If he did, I was ready!

"So Jakey, how's my uncle Arnie treating your mom? Good?" Anthony asked.

Jake shrugged and looked at his toes. "I guess."

"You know, come to think of it, you're a guy that could maybe help me out," said Anthony.

"I am?" said Jake.

"Absolutely. Me and Richie might have some work for you. You're a helpful kind of kid, right? You do good, there could be cash involved."

"Cash? Yeah—I mean . . . help you out how?" Jake asked.

"Delivery work. Easy peasy."

Talking, the two boys stopped paying attention to Luca and me. My leash went slack, and I edged closer. The big dog's ears were up, and so was his tail. Now at last I had my chance, and I gave him a friendly head butt. He replied by stomping his forepaws and bumping me with his snout—a blow that sent me halfway across the sidewalk.

I shook myself and charged back for more. The big baby! He didn't even know his own strength.

"Ya wanna play?" I asked.

"Yeah!"

I rolled over, jumped to my feet, charged forward and grabbed him around the neck. He froze to let me get a good long sniff.

"What's your den like?" I wanted to know. "Smells like you eat pretty good, and there're lots of humans there. I hope the others are nicer than this nasty one."

Before the pit bull could reply, Jake and Anthony were pulling us apart.

"Are you okay, Strudel?" Jake asked. "Did he bite you?"

"Hey-ey-ey, Luca—don't hurt that wiener dog. It ain't his fault he's undersized." Anthony yanked the leash hard, and Luca, unprepared, lost his balance and slid a couple of feet.

Ouch.

I barked a sympathy bark.

Jake misunderstood. *"No,* Strudel! You don't want to annoy that dog. He's a lot bigger than you."

Anthony tugged the leash again, laughed and started to walk away. "I'll be in touch, Little Jakey. Meantime, watch out that that big, scary dog'a yours don't hurt nobody." He raised one hand without looking back. He was still chuckling.

A block later we ran into Rudy, the poodle. He turned out to be black and to have legs as long as mine are short. Unfortunately, he smelled like—*phew*—shampoo.

"Hey! Hey! Hey! Thanks for the food. It was top of the line!" I told him.

"Sorry about the stink," he apologized. "I just got back from the groomer."

"Buddy, I feel your pain," I said.

Lisa and Jake talked about school for a little while. Then Lisa said, "We were on our way to the dog park. Do you want to come? Your new dog is cute."

Jake said, "Sure, I guess. Is that okay with you, Strudel?"

Yeah, yeah, totally! I love the dog park!

Lisa laughed. "That tail wag looks like a yes to me."

The four of us, two dogs, two humans, fell in together. Jake asked Lisa if she thought I'd be okay with the other dogs there. "Strudel's pretty small, I guess," Jake said.

Lisa laughed. "He's exactly the size he's supposed to be. And he'll totally be fine. Look at the way Rudy acts with him. Even though Rudy's bigger, Strudel's the alpha dog."

"What's an alpha dog?" Jake asked.

"Like, the dog in charge," Lisa said. "Rudy's a big wimp, aren't you, Rudy-wugs? But I still wuv you, yes I do." The way she talked made me think of Maisie. Her human's granddaughter used to put baby clothes on her. Maisie told me they squeezed in all the wrong places, but she didn't mind. It was an easy way to make a human happy.

"You're lucky you're too big for baby clothes," I told Rudy.

"Yeah, but you should see the sweater she makes me wear at Christmas," Rudy said.

The dog park was next to a children's playground, one additional long block away. Four dogs were romping already when we got there, all of them recognizable from the smells they had left at the power pole. Lisa opened a metal gate to let us in, then she unclipped Rudy's leash and Jake unclipped mine.

"Don't get into trouble," Jake told me, and I could tell he was anxious. He didn't realize that to me these dogs weren't strangers. Through our messaging system, we'd already sorted out a way to get along.

That's why I walked in like I owned the place.

"Hey, hey, hey, new dog!" said a miniature pinscher.

"Good to see ya!" said another pit bull, this one silver-gray and a lot leggier than Luca.

"Great to be here," I said. "Great to have a home at last. I guess you know I've been in a shelter."

"Yeah, that's tough," said the min pin. "I've been around a shelter or two myself."

Rudy poked his nose in my face. "We better get some running in now. My human never lets me stay here long. She's always got homework. Race ya to the fence—let's go!"

If it had been a digging race, I would have won paws down. But running is not my long suit, so to speak, and Rudy beat me to the fence by a mile. To even things out, I staged a sneak attack, rolled right under him and popped up on the other side.

"Nice move," he said.

"It's a doxie thing," I said.

After that, we both tumbled around, getting good and dirty.

"That oughta help the smell some," I told him.

"I hope so," he said. "Talk about embarrassing."

"Hey"—I remembered something—"what's this Pier 67 Gang, anyway? There were warnings about it at message central."

The mood at the dog park had been all carefree lolling and wagging, but now it changed. The min pin stopped in his tracks and growled. A golden retriever dropped down and tried to hide under a bench. Rudy himself looked right and left, then stretched his legs, ready to run.

"I don't even like to talk about them," said the gray pit bull. "But if you must know, they are"—she lowered her voice—"*cats.*"

"*Cats?*" I howled.

"Shhhh!" said the pit bull, and the other dogs echoed her: "Shhhh!"

"These are not just ordinary cats," said the min pin. "Ordinary cats we can handle, no problem. But the Pier 67 Gang—they are evil, pure and simple. And they've got the kills to prove it."

Eleven

Soon after that, Lisa announced that she had to go. Walking home with Jake, I should have been perfectly content. My new neighborhood boasted enough smells to entertain a dog for a lifetime. The dogs at the dog park were friendly, and they recognized my superior qualities.

There was just one problem: a gang of evil and murderous cats.

It sounded like somebody's idea of a joke. But those dogs weren't joking.

What should I do about this gang? Was it possible to keep away from them? What would Chief do?

These questions were in my head when we got home, and I trotted over to the plastic cereal bowls they'd put on the floor for me. The food one was empty, but there was plenty of water. I guessed I would know I really had a forever home when my humans remembered to feed me.

I sighed and rested my head on my paws. For the next few minutes, I forgot about evil cats and thought instead of my previous human. Every afternoon he used to go to the kitchen, remove three butter cookies from a blue tin, eat two of them with a glass of milk, and split the third one with me.

Some days he gave me the whole cookie for myself.

Those were very good days.

I missed him—and not just the kibble and the cookies, either. He had loved me and petted me and patiently taught me tricks. For an energetic dog, it had been a quiet life. But up till the calamity, it had been comfortable and safe as well.

My thoughts were interrupted by the sound of the patio door sliding open and Mutanski coming into the kitchen.

"Jake! Get your body out here and take a look. You'll never believe what the stupid mutt did!" She wagged her finger at me. "Bad dog! *Baaad* dog!"

Bad dog . . . *what?*

Then I remembered. She must have found the snake!

This day had been so eventful, I'd entirely forgotten it. But why did Mutanski sound mad? Shouldn't I be getting a reward? How about a cookie?

After all, I had saved my family from certain slithering death!

Jake came into the kitchen shaking his head. "If there's another mess, just tell me. You don't have to get all dramatic."

"It's way worse than a mess," said Mutanski. "He chewed up the garden hose—destroyed it totally!"

Garden hose? What's garden hose? *I never heard of this thing called* garden hose.

All of us went out to the patio, where the green snake remained as dead as ever, its mangled carcass in half a thousand pieces. Jake slapped his head with both hands. "Oh, Strudel, noooo! Why did you do that?"

To answer the question, I re-enacted the epic struggle: I stomped my front paws; I growled; I grabbed what was left of the snake by the throat and *shook!*

Mutanski laughed. "I guess you showed *it,* right, Strudel?"

I sure did! Yes I did!

"How much do hoses cost?" Jake asked.

"A lot," said Mutanski.

Now I sensed I might have miscalculated. Was I in trouble? Just in case, I wagged my tail, sat back and held out my paw to shake.

Jake took my paw and sighed. "I guess you're worth it, Strudel. I'll get a broom and a trash bag."

A few minutes later Mom got home. She barely had time to unbutton her coat before Mutanski told her about the garden hose. Apparently garden hoses are less dangerous than rattlesnakes, but to this day I am not sure why that is.

"I'll pay for it, Mom," Jake said. "You can take it out of my allowance."

"He's already lost his allowance for, like, the next year, hasn't he, Mom?" Mutanski asked.

Mom turned to face the two of them. "Just once I'd like to walk in the door and hear my two happy children say, 'Welcome home, Mother dear!'"

"Sorry," said Jake and Mutanski at the same time.

"There's no money in the budget for a new hose, so I guess we use the watering can," Mom went on. "And Jake, if you're going to keep this dog—emphasis on the *if*—then it looks like you'll have to earn some money of your own. Arnie's right. Dogs are expensive. Even the small bag of food I bought today set me back some bucks. There wasn't enough left to buy beer."

"Ohhh, *poor* Arnie!" Mutanski threw her head back,

slapped her forehead and moaned. "Forced to buy his own beer!"

Mom exhaled sharply. "That's about enough of that, young lady."

"Suits me," said Mutanski, and she stomped out of the room.

Mom watched Mutanski's retreating back.

Jake spoke quietly. "Strudel is my dog, Mom. We are going to keep him."

Mom turned and looked at Jake. "What? Oh, right—the dog. Honey, if you want to keep him, you will have to step up and earn some money."

It doesn't take a dachshund long to identify which humans belong in his pack. Jake was a member of mine, and so was Mutanski, even if she didn't want to admit it.

As for Mom, if she wanted to join, she still had to prove herself. The bag of kibble she bought was a start. And Grandpa seemed like he might be okay. He was the one who had pointed out that a dog needs to eat.

Then there was Arnie: Strudel Enemy No. 1. No way could he join. In fact, I steered clear of him anytime he visited. That night, he didn't come to dinner, and Jake took advantage of the opportunity to drop me a piece of hot dog.

It's true I prefer it without mustard, but it was the thought that counted.

After dinner, Mom reminded Jake about homework, and Jake started to argue. Then he remembered he was supposed to be on his best behavior.

"Absolutely, Mom! I'm on it!"

Mom rolled her eyes. "Okay, kiddo, don't get carried away being good. I won't recognize you."

Twelve

During the next few weeks, I stayed out of trouble.

Mostly.

There was that unfortunate incident on the night they call Halloween. What is that holiday about, anyway? Children who smelled like sugar and looked like monsters rang our doorbell one after another and—here's the really bad part—they stole our candy!

Oh no! Oh no! Danger!

I barked so much I lost my voice.

Later, to recover my strength, I ate every last sugar-coated wrapper I could steal out of Jake's wastebasket. When I woke up in the middle of the night with a tummy ache, I found out Jake was awake with a tummy ache, too.

That night we both left multicolor messes on the rug.

The next morning Mutanski thought this was hilarious.

Mom did not.

Other than that, I began to think I really had found a forever home. There were no butter cookies, but meals became regular. Jake took me out in the morning and at night. After school every day, he took me for a good long walk. A lot of times he and Lisa took me and Rudy to the dog park, where I met the rest of the neighborhood dogs. Sometimes I saw Luca on Jake's and my walks, but we never had a chance to talk. Jake and Anthony kept us far apart.

As for the Pier 67 Gang, they stayed out of sight. Maybe they weren't as bad as every dog said. Or maybe they were unusually smart for cats, smart enough to know you don't mess with a dachshund.

As for that other dirty rotten bad guy—Arnie—he scolded Mom for buying dog food instead of beer, she snapped at him and he took his anger out on me. When he thought no one was looking, he aimed a kick, but, being a klutz, he missed me by a mile.

Not taking any chances, I kept out of his way after that and learned to like Fridays, when Grandpa came over and Arnie did not. On Fridays I stuck like glue under Jake's chair, waiting for the odd bit of sausage pizza to fall my way. One week Grandpa asked about me. "How's Killer settling in?"

Jake said, "Good."

Mutanski said, "Arnie hates him."

"That's a point in Killer's favor, then," said Grandpa.

Mom sighed. "Dad, could you please give it a rest? My personal life is my business."

For a few moments, the only sounds were the sounds of chewing. Then Grandpa shifted in his chair. "Speaking of personal life, I've been meaning to tell you that, uh . . . well, you're not the only grown-up around here that's got one."

This time when Mom spoke, there was a smile in her voice. "Really, Dad? Go on. I'm all ears."

"Well, uh . . . lately," Grandpa said, "I've been watching TV a couple nights a week with Betty Rossi."

"Who's Betty Rossi?" Jake asked.

Mutanski said, "From Betty's Quik-Stop, right? That's cool, Grandpa. She always used to give me and Jake Life Savers when you or Grandma took us there."

"How did you happen to run into her, Dad?" Mom asked.

"She's sewing costumes for the Mummers," said Grandpa. "Her boy Ray's marching with the Frogs this year."

"Oh—the mummers brigade you're a marshal for," Mom said. "Ray was a troublemaker in high school. So was his brother."

"Not anymore," said Grandpa. "Ray's a police officer, and Tommy works for a trucking company. They both finished college."

"And I didn't," Mom said. "You never miss a chance to point that out."

Grandpa pushed his chair back. "I didn't mean anything."

"Oh?" said Mom. "Then why bring it up?"

Two more things happened during the first few weeks at Jake's house: I learned about video games, and my memory of the calamity began to come back.

Jake played video games most nights after his homework was done. That means he sat on the sofa with a plastic controller in his hands, and he pressed buttons on it and waved it around.

There are many mysteries about humans, and video games is one.

The video game Jake played most was loud and ugly. The first time I was around it, I had another of those flashback events and started to tremble. Jake was so busy he didn't notice until I scrambled under the coffee table to hide.

"Is it too loud, Strudel?" he asked. "Here, I'll put on headphones."

Without taking his eyes from the TV, Jake scratched my back one-handed—*awww*—and then fiddled with some cords. The TV went silent. When I calmed down I worked up the courage to look again.

In front of me on the screen, buildings were blowing up, humans were shooting with guns and falling down; bombs and tanks flashed and flamed.

Suddenly a few scattered memories from the night of the calamity came back. It was an awful *boom* that had awakened me from sound sleep on my soft, familiar pillow. After that there had been more booms, each one of which seemed to echo in my skull, and then came flashes of unnatural light throwing black shadows on the wall.

Terrified, I had leaped off my pillow and run around my home, searching everywhere for a place to hide, but no corner was safe from the awful noise and light. I howled and howled and no one came to help. The pain in my head was awful. I had no choice—I had to escape!

In desperation, I threw myself against a window screen, which tore with the force of my body's impact.

I was free!

But no . . . the screen's sharp corner had caught my collar. For anguished moments I struggled and whined, until finally the collar broke and I dropped a few feet to the hard, wet ground outside.

I thought I had escaped, but I was wrong. The terrifying noise and light continued. Worse yet, it was raining. I saw tree branches whipping and waving in the wind, and the oncoming headlights of cars. I heard brakes squealing, and the bone-rattling booms all around.

I ran across the boulevard near my home. I ran toward

tall buildings in the city. The more I ran, the quieter it was. Finally the flashing sky grew dark.

Jake's video game was called *Random Apocalypse*. *Apocalypse* means the end of the world. Had I endured an apocalypse myself?

And what had happened to my former human?

Each night after video games, I had two more jobs to do: listen to Jake talk before he fell asleep, and lick his face if he was sad.

Sometimes the things Jake told me were like stories. But his were different from Chief's. There was not necessarily a hero or a happy ending. Peace and justice did not always triumph.

From Jake I learned that Grandpa worked in a bakery, and sometimes Jake helped out. The job he liked best was making an Italian pastry called cannoli that's stuffed with sweet creamy cheese.

I learned about Jake's dad, too. His name was Tyler and he lived in Germany. He was serving with the United States Army. He and Jake's mom had been a couple for a while, but they never got married.

Jake heard from his dad on his birthday and Christmas. Usually there was a funny card and money in an envelope, usually twenty dollars.

Jake told me he was worried about the money he owed his mom for the garden hose. He hoped his dad would come through with cash at Christmas. Otherwise, maybe Anthony would give him the job he had talked about that time.

"I'm a little scared of Anthony," Jake said, "but I would take his money."

Thirteen

The weather got colder. Most days I was allowed to stay indoors when Jake and Mutanski went to school. Then one night Mutanski left the bathroom door open, and I ate a half roll of toilet paper for a snack. Catching it and killing it was fun, but the taste left something to be desired. Anyway, the next morning, Mom shut me out on the patio "just to be on the safe side."

Luckily the sky was clear, and Jake had positioned my pillow in a sunny spot. After I made my usual rounds, I dozed off thinking about my previous human. What had happened to him during the apocalypse? Was he up in heaven missing me? Could he look down and see that I was happy?

I hoped so.

After a while, my nap was disturbed by a stomach-churning odor, the putrid unmentionable stench of (please forgive my language) *cat*!

My first thought was for my food dish.

I opened my eyes and saw my worst nightmare come true: A cat as big as a fox terrier had his face in my dish and was chowing down as if he had every right to be there!

Faster than you can say "Get away from my food, you flea-brained feline!" I was on my feet snapping and growling, a display of canine firepower that should have sent the intruder fleeing in terror. . . .

But it did not.

Instead, the cat looked up lazily, wiped a paw over one eye, licked his whiskers, blinked and said, "My dear dog, do please quiet down."

His voice was low and smooth and creepy. My hackles were up, but I felt a chill. There was only one explanation: the Pier 67 Gang.

"Your humans ought to buy you a better brand of chow," he continued. "If I were you, I'd be shopping for a new and improved family."

Oh, now *that* was just insulting!

So what if the gang's fearsome reputation was everywhere? The trouble was obvious. No one had taught this cat a lesson! Without further ado, I went straight for his fat, furry throat.

Only instead of the satisfying crunch of feline bone and flesh, I felt a piercing pain in my right flank, followed by a piercing pain in my left.

Owwww! I howled and spun on my toenails. Behind me I saw—this was not good—two emaciated cats, one young, sleek and black, the other white, one-eyed and filthy. Both had my blood on their claws. Both were singing evil, ululating feline songs.

Both were ready to strike again.

A single cat is no match for a dog, but now I confronted three—all of them tough, ugly strays hardened from life on the streets. The gashes on my backside stung like fire. I wanted more than anything to check out the damage, do a little licking, get some relief from the pain . . . but I dared not let down my guard.

"All right, boys, that will do," said the big cat, the one apparently in charge. He was delicately removing bits of *my* food from his whiskers with a claw. "If we hurt him too badly, the humans will know we've been here, and there might be complications. Now go ahead and eat your share of the spoils. Don't ever let it be said that I am greedy."

While his henchmen finished off my kibble, the boss washed up. All I could do was watch in misery.

At this, finished eating, the black cat licked his lips and spoke for the first time. "I guess you've heard of the Pier 67 Gang?" My patio had been invaded and my backside bloodied. My stomach was empty. Still, I had my pride. "Nope," I said. "I never have."

These words were hardly out of my mouth when, from behind me, I heard a rustling sound.

What now?

Warily, I looked around and saw a terrifying sight: cat eyes, an entire constellation, glowing hot in the leafy gloom of the boxwood hedge.

At last my courage failed. "H-h-how many of you are there?"

"Enough," the boss replied coolly. "And now, my dear dog, we need a favor. From this point forward, please leave your food for us. We may not stop by every day. We have a variety of dining options. But when we're in the neighborhood, we will expect to enjoy your ungrudging hospitality."

"H-h-how did you even know I was here?" I asked.

"One of my patrol sentries got a whiff of your food this morning," the cat said. "He reported to a lieutenant, the lieutenant reported to me. Our feline network is extensive and unstoppable. You'll forgive me, but I've forgotten your name. It's something sweet, is it not? Cupcake? Dumpling? Doughnut?"

I would have given anything not to answer, but I still felt the painful sting of feline claws. "My human calls me Strudel," I said.

"Strudel!" There was a chorus of ugly feline laughter.

"What's *your* name?" I asked the boss, trying to change the subject.

The big cat swished his tail. "You may call me Capo, director-in-charge of the Pier 67 Gang. My associates here are Lamar and Pepito. And just so you don't forget, here is something to remember us by."

Capo blinked at the black cat, Lamar, who unsheathed his cruel claws with blinding speed and raked my unprotected nose.

I couldn't help it. I squealed, *"Aiii!"*

Lamar removed a drop of my blood from his paw with a delicate flick of his tongue. "You want I should do it again?" he asked Capo.

"Not now," said Capo. "It's time we moved on. But do not worry, my dear dog. We will return soon to sample your hospitality. We would never want you to be lonely."

Fourteen

I turned to watch the three cats depart. Lamar sat back on his haunches, gracefully leaped over the hedge and landed lightly on a wooden crossbar of the fence. There he balanced for an instant before climbing up and over.

Pepito, the scruffy white cat, did the same thing, but it wasn't nearly as pretty. Capo did not make the jump to the crossbar at all. Instead, he slinked through a gap in the hedge. The last I saw of him was the jet-black tip of his tail.

As for the other cats, the ones whose eyes I had seen in the gloom, they had vanished without a sound.

Grateful to be alone, I took a deep breath, circled twice and dropped down on my pillow.

This would never have happened to Chief, I thought. Chief would have taken on those cats and dispatched them three at a time.

But I wasn't Chief, was I? I was frightened, bloodied, hungry and humiliated.

I was also puzzled about one thing. How did Capo get in and out of my domain, anyway? He was too fat for jumping.

To find out, I left my pillow and trotted to the gap in the hedge. Here my short legs were an advantage. Bending my knees and elbows, I forced my way beneath the foliage and inch by inch moved forward.

I couldn't see well in the shadows, and the twigs and branches scraped my back, especially—*ouch*—the tender places the cats had scratched. But, true to my determined hound-dog nature, I kept going until finally my nose bumped something solid—the wooden fence.

There had to be an opening somewhere. I twisted my neck until I saw it—a hole created by a rotted section of board less than a foot above my head. A loose-limbed, squishy-bodied cat—even a fat one—could squeeze between hedge and fence, then wriggle through the hole. My own canine physique, on the other hand, was too sturdy for that kind of contortion.

Covered with dirt and leaves, I backed out from under the hedge. I had answered my own question. I had found Capo's entrance and exit.

But so what? I had no way to keep the cats from returning, and when they did I would be at their mercy.

When Mutanski got home, she washed me gently with shampoo (*bleah!*), then doctored my wounds with a spray that made my nose and backside sting all over again.

I knew she was trying to help, but this was awful!

I bore up bravely till finally she toweled me off and set me free. Then I scooted away fast and sat down by the front door to wait for Jake.

He was carrying a paper bag when he came in. He had

a big smile on his face . . . till he saw me. "Oh my gosh, Strudel, what happened?"

Mutanski, lying on the sofa watching TV, spoke without looking up. "I think he went after something by the fence, and the boxwood bushes scratched him. He was dirty and bloody and sad when I got home."

"You cleaned him up?" Jake said.

"Yeah, well." Mutanski glanced at her brother. "I didn't think you'd do it right." Her lips were gold that day, and in spite of the cool weather, she was wearing shorts and sandals. Her toenail polish matched her lips.

"Yeah, I would've," Jake said, "but thanks."

Mutanski shrugged. "Whatever. What's in the bag?"

"Present for Strudel. Maybe this'll make you feel better, buddy. Look!"

When I saw what was inside, I forgot how bad I felt and spun myself dizzy. Then I made a round-the-world circuit of the living room—sofa, coffee table, plaid chair and back.

Thank you! Thank you! Thank you! Thank you! Thank you! Thank you!

"I think he likes them," said Mutanski.

Oh boy, oh boy, oh boy! Do I!

They were the most beautiful objects ever, my very own dog dishes at last—white and made of pottery, with blue paw prints for decoration. The days of plastic cereal bowls were over. I was a real member of the family now!

"Where'd ya get the money?" Mutanski asked.

"I did like Mom said. I got an odd job," Jake said. "I paid her back for the garden hose, too."

"The job must be super odd if they hired you. Hey, wait"— now Mutanski turned her head to look at her brother—"this doesn't have anything to do with that Anthony kid, Arnie's nephew, does it?"

Jake frowned. "What if it does?"

"Look, little bro," Mutanski said, "I can't tell you what to do. But just be careful. He and his homey Richie both, they are bad news."

That night when Jake climbed into bed, I curled up on the pillow by his head. But instead of telling me about himself, he said, "How about if we read some Chief, Strudel? My teacher's been bugging me to read more. And besides, I don't feel that much like talking. There's so much stuff buzzing around my head, I wouldn't know where to start."

Chief, Dog of the Old West

On the day the bank was robbed, Sheriff Silver's rooster awoke with the sun: cock-a-doodle-doo!

The sleeping square-jawed sheriff opened his eyes and sighed. "I hate that bird."

At breakfast time the happy homestead was further disturbed when leading townsperson Millie Bly Bumsted burst in the front door, hollering, "The bank's been robbed! The bank's been robbed!"

Sheriff Silver was seated at the kitchen table, coffee cup in hand. "We heard you the first time," he said.

And Chef Pierre added, "In France, the tradition is knock first, enter later."

"There ain't no time for niceties now," said Millie Bly Bumsted. "The dirty rotten polecats were last seen riding out of town. If you hurry, you can cut them off at the pass!"

"Which pass did you have in mind?" asked Sheriff Silver.

"Any ol' pass! Now hop to, Sheriff! My savings are in that bank and so are yours!"

Recollecting that Millie Bly Bumsted was right, Sheriff Silver leaped to his feet, at the same time dropping his coffee cup, which hit the pine-plank floor and smashed.

"Second one this week," Chef Pierre observed.

"Never mind coffee cups!" Sheriff Silver said stoutly. "There are miscreants to catch and cash dollars to recover!"

In a trice, the sheriff had strapped on his holster and affixed his silver star to his vest. "Ready, Chief?" He looked to his faithful dog.

Woof, said Chief.

And out the door they dashed.

Many anxious hours passed around the old home place till at last a downcast and dejected Sheriff Silver returned. Behind him came his faithful dog, ears and tail drooping.

"What can be the matter, Pa?" asked brainy, blue-eyed Rachel Mae. "Is it possible you've failed?"

"Both possible and a fact," said Sheriff Silver. "At Deadhead Swamp, the trail went cold."

"Do not despair!" said Rachel Mae. "I will devise a plan!"

Sheriff Silver's smile was wan. "You do that, Rachel Mae."

The sheriff's daughter sat down with her pencil. Sheriff Silver sat down with a cup of tea. Chief took to his bed and cogitated. His keen nose had failed him. Now how would he locate the bad guys' lair?

What was needed was a bird's-eye view.

And come to think of it, Chief knew just the bird.

Jake read the first sentence of the next chapter, but a big yawn cut the second sentence short, and he closed the book. "I'm too sleepy to keep reading, Strudel. But what do you think? Will Chief and the sheriff find the hideout?"

I had a feeling they would, and wagged my tail to show it.

Also, Chief had given me an idea.

Fifteen

The weather stayed good the next day, and I was put out on the patio. As usual, I had a bowl of kibble, but the thought of those glowing cat eyes kept me from eating so much as a morsel . . . no matter how my stomach protested.

Part of the neighborhood's regular background noise was the coo of pigeons. Having lived all my life in the city, I was used to it and rarely paid attention. Birds, as everyone knows, are unreasonable and silly and not worth your time.

Now, though, thanks to Chief, I realized birds might have their uses.

Roughly twenty feet above me on the power line sat four pigeons. I had never spoken to a bird before, but fear of the cats made me desperate.

"Excuse me," I woofed. "Feathered friends? Does one of you have a minute to spare? The truth is"—admitting this was embarrassing—"I could use your help."

This got the pigeons' attention, and a small hen answered: "With what, dog, our help with what?"

It is obvious to dogs that birds are our inferiors, so I had assumed that birds knew it, too, and would greet me with appropriate respect. "Esteemed canine" would have been nice and "Mr. Dog" acceptable, but plain old "dog"? That was just bad manners.

Still, I needed a favor. "If you don't mind coming down here," I went on, "I will tell you. It shouldn't take much of your time."

The pigeons responded with a burst of staccato cooing that sounded suspiciously like laughter. First the cats had laughed at me, now this. Were the ants in their anthill laughing at me, too?

"Word on the wire says you've got cat trouble, that's the word," the small hen said.

I was astonished. "How do you know?"

The second pigeon answered. "We make it our business to know."

"But we don't gossip," the third pigeon added.

"Never gossip, never." The small hen turned her head to consult with the other three. "Shall I chance it with this dog? Chance it, you think?"

"See what he wants, but don't get too close," the second bird advised.

The small hen dropped from the wire, spread her wings and glided to a landing on the picnic bench above me. When I jumped up and leaned my paws on the bench's edge, we were eye-to-beady-eye. I could see the hen was nervous. The pulse in her throat beat fast.

She was also surprisingly pretty, with lustrous gray feathers, brilliant red feet and a snazzy purple rainbow on her neck.

"I'll get right to the point," I said. "Where is the Pier 67 Gang's hideout?"

Above us, the pigeon chorus fluttered their wings and coo-coo-cooed. Were they still laughing? But the small hen only bobbed her head. She seemed to be more curteous than the others.

"Pay them no mind," she said. "What's obvious from the sky may not be obvious from the ground. The cats' hideout is at Pier 67, the 67th pier down on the river."

If a dog could blush, I would have. Where else but Pier 67 would the Pier 67 Gang's hideout be?

Not that I knew where Pier 67 was or, for that matter, *what* it was.

The pigeon hen seemed to sense both my embarrassment and my ignorance. "Pier 67 is on the Delaware River. Ships used to dock there but they don't anymore. The wicked cats have taken it over, those wicked wicked cats."

"And how far away is Pier 67?" I asked.

"As the pigeon flies?" the hen asked. "It's half a mile, half a mile, not more. Those that travel on paws not wings would find it somewhat farther."

Above us, the pigeons on the wire continued titter-cooing. "Thank you for not laughing," I told the small hen. "I really appreciate your help."

"*De nada*, it's nothing, it's *niente*," she said. "We birds know a lot, you know."

"What more can you tell me about the cats?" I asked.

The pigeon hen marched in place, turned full circle and pecked at something in her feathers. Then she settled in as if she had a story.

"The cats sleep in boxes brought by foolish humans; foolish humans bring bags of cat food, too. But it's never enough, for the cats it's insufficient. They gobble that food then gobble up more—the pups, chicks and eggs from every nest. In their wake they leave a trail of blood, only a bloody trail. They're hated and feared by the riverbank creatures, for they not only kill, they torture.

"It's rumored they have no souls!"

Her words made me think of those glowing eyes, and I shuddered.

What might those cats be capable of?

"I just have one more question," I said after a moment. "The broken slat in my back fence leaves a hole that's open to the alley. Is that how Capo gets in and out?"

"That's it, the hole in the fence, that's it." The small hen bobbed her head. "But he'll be stuck if he gets fatter than he already is—any fatter and he'll get stuck. Is that all you want to know, you know? I have flying to do today, flying and spying to do today."

"Yes, thank you, Miss Bird," I said. "I hope I wasn't rude before. I see that till now, I did not have proper appreciation of your kind."

"Nor I of yours, I'm sure," said the bird politely. "The name's Johanna, by the way. And yours is Strudel, I think?"

Without waiting for my answer, the pigeon looked toward the sky and flapped her wings. "We birds don't like cats either," she cooed as she rose to join her friends. "Perhaps we ought to form an alliance."

As I watched Johanna depart, I felt a peculiar sensation. For the first time in my life, I envied a creature that wasn't a dog. If I could fly, those cats wouldn't stand a chance.

Sixteen

I felt better after I talked to the pigeon, but not for long. How was I going to use the information she provided? I didn't have a plan. Unlike Rachel Mae, I didn't even have a pencil.

All day I stared forlornly at the food in my dish, fearing what the cats would do to me if I ate it. By late afternoon I was so hungry there was only one thought left in my head: Any dog afraid of cats is a disgrace to his species.

That day the cats never showed, and when Mutanski came home from school she was surprised to find my food dish full.

"You okay, Strudel?" She gave me a belly rub—*awwww*. "Not getting sick, are ya?"

Mutanski's lipstick was black, and so were her fingernails. She looked like one of the evildoers in *Random Apocalypse*. But she smelled normal. And she brought my food inside for me. Safe in the kitchen, I settled down, ate lunch at last and felt much better.

Then Jake got home, and he had bought me another present—a red rubber porcupine that squeaked if you bit it hard.

"What do you think, Stru?" He threw it for me to catch.

What do I think? *Oh boy! Oh boy! Oh boy! Who cares about cats? Come on, let's play!*

But Mutanski was determined to spoil our fun. "What odd job did you have to do to buy that?" she asked her brother.

If Jake answered, I didn't hear. My new toy was pretty loud. I dropped it at Jake's feet, and Mutanski asked another question: "Do you know what those guys are up to? Something sketchy, I bet."

Jake picked up the porcupine but didn't throw it. "Lay off me, wouldja? Come on, Strudel. Time for a good long walk."

That day was Thursday, and Arnie came over for dinner. He had his own key so, as usual, he came in through the front door and hollered hello.

Mom wasn't home. Jake answered, "Hello," from the kitchen. Mutanski, next to me on the living room sofa, didn't answer at all. Arnie usually got a can of beer from the fridge, then sat in the kitchen till Mom arrived. For weeks, I had stayed out of his way by keeping to the living room anytime he was over. According to Mutanski, Arnie had no attention span and a faulty memory. If I was lucky, he had forgotten I even existed.

Unfortunately, what happened next reminded him.

Crossing toward the kitchen, Arnie stepped on my red porcupine toy, which went *squeeeeak,* causing Arnie to jump—"A mouse!"—and step on Jake's shoes, and then . . . fall over backward. It truly takes a unique talent to be laid low by a pair of shoes, but this was just the kind of talent Arnie possessed.

From her spot next to me, Mutanski had seen the whole thing. Arnie started to curse; she started to laugh.

"It's not a mouse, it's a dog toy!" Mutanski said. Then she grabbed the porcupine from the floor and waved it in Arnie's face.

Scowling, Arnie got to his feet and rubbed the seat of his pants. "Who the heck has spare cash for dog toys in this house, I'd like to know? Especially toys for a sissy dog like that one."

"He is not a sissy dog, and don't call him that," said Mutanski.

Thank you, Mutanski.

"Sissy dog, sissy dog, sissy dog!" Arnie repeated.

"You know what I admire about you most, Arnie?" Mutanski faced him, her hands on her hips.

"What?" he asked.

"Your impressive level of maturity," said Mutanski.

"Uhhh, thanks," said Arnie. "I think."

"Yeah, you do that if you can," said Mutanski.

"Do what?" Arnie asked.

"*Think*," said Mutanski.

Arnie frowned, opened his mouth to say something, changed his mind and returned to his original plan—getting himself a beer. Soon after that, Mom arrived home. She made meat loaf for dinner, and at the table Arnie brought up dogs again. I was in the living room as usual, but I could hear the conversation.

"If you gotta have a dog, it oughta be a *real* dog. Like my nephew Anthony's dog, Luca."

"Luca is a very pretty dog," said Mom.

"Pretty?" Arnie snorted. "He's strong as a bull and fierce when he has to be—he's *the enforcer!*"

Fierce? What a joke! Luca is the biggest sissy dog I know.

Mom said, "Enforcer of what?"

"Let's just say that Luca helps Anthony and his pal Richie with their business," Arnie said.

"I wasn't aware they had a business," Mom said. "They're only thirteen. What kind of business is it?"

"Yeah," Mutanski joined in. "Jake and I have been wondering the same thing."

"Leave me out of this!" said Jake.

There was a pause. Maybe Arnie was chewing. Then he said, "Sales, I guess you'd call it. And the presence of Luca keeps certain people from trying to take advantage."

"I don't like the sound of this," said Mom. "Are you encouraging those boys? What are they selling?"

"Nothing that's strictly illegal," said Arnie. "You might call it participation in the great American free enterprise system. Some other kids I know might learn from their example."

He meant Jake and Mutanski. Even I, the dog in the other room, knew that. Mutanski's reply was a grunt, and Jake's was to shift his feet.

Jake wasn't talkative that night before bed, either. Instead, he pulled *Chief* off the bookshelf and settled back against his pillow. When I curled up beside him, I closed my eyes and imagined the story like a show on TV playing out before me.

Chief, Dog of the Old West

Rachel Mae's plan required Sheriff Silver and Chef Pierre to travel by hot-air balloon across Deadhead Swamp, spot the hideout with a spyglass and drop a net on the bank robbers to trap them.

"But, darlin'," Sheriff Silver said, "there's not a hot-air balloon within a thousand miles o' Groovers Gulch."

"Nor net nor spyglass neither," added Chef Pierre.

"These items can be ordered from Sears and Roebuck, then delivered by Wells Fargo stage," Rachel Mae said. "I have taken the liberty of dog-earing the pages in the catalog."

"Alas," said her father sadly, "by the time the order arrives, the outlaws will be halfway to Abilene."

Rachel Mae never did cotton to being contradicted. Her retort was pert indeed, but no one heard it over the sound of the mournful howl that at that moment pierced the night.

"A werewolf!" cried Sheriff Silver from his hiding place under the table.

Chef Pierre peered out the window. "It is but our faithful canine, Chief. He is howling at la lune."

Chef Pierre was not entirely right. It was Chief's mournful howl they heard. But la lune, that is the moon, was not its object. Rather, it was a passing eagle he'd met some months before when their interests aligned over a prairie dog. Acquaintance renewed, Chief and the eagle conducted a confab, the results of which were to play out the next day.

Even before the rooster crowed the next morning, Chief was rested and raring to go.

Seeing his eagerness, Sheriff Silver announced: "The canine has a plan."

"Oh fine," said Rachel Mae. "Go with your dog and not your daughter."

"There, there, mademoiselle," said Chef Pierre. "Eat some oatmeal, and you'll feel better."

Meanwhile, Sheriff Silver saddled up and headed out with Chief in the lead. What the sheriff never noticed was the silhouette of an eagle flying high above them in the azure sky and pointing the way.

That evening, as the setting sun made peppermint stripes of the clouds, Sheriff Silver and Chief returned home, battered but triumphant.

"Pa, I have ordered the balloon and the spyglass and the net," said Rachel Mae by way of greeting. "They will be here in six months."

"No need for all that now," said the sheriff. "Thanks to Chief, the bank robbers are locked up tight, and the townsfolk's savings are secure."

"C'est merveilleux!" said Chef Pierre. "What happened?"

Sheriff Silver rubbed the manly stubble on his chin. "I reckon I'll never rightly understand just how my faithful canine accomplished it. But this morning he led me straightaway across Deadhead Swamp, and thereafter on a zigzag track through the badlands until at last we reached the outlaws' hideout in the rocks.

"Fortunately, I had taken the preemptive precaution of recruiting a posse of leading townsfolk. With the element of surprise on our side, we soon had the robbers surrounded. Seeing the situation was hopeless, those outlaws surrendered without so much as a wasted bullet. Now the gang awaits swift frontier justice in the hoosegow."

"Vive le *Chief!*" cried Chef Pierre.

And even Rachel Mae had to admit that the canine had done his job well. Besides, she had her hot-air balloon, her spyglass and her net to look forward to. Surely they would come in handy for something.

Jake closed the book, put it back on the shelf, then scratched me on the back. "What do you think, Strudel? Could a dog and an eagle really be friends?"

I was lying on Jake's pillow with my tail squished against the wall. There was no space for wagging, but I managed a wiggle.

Sure! Sure! Sure, they could! Why not? I made friends with a pigeon, didn't I?

Seventeen

With winter on the way, the next few days were gray, damp and cold.

Yessss!

Bad weather meant I could stay indoors during the day—safe, warm and well-fed.

Unfortunately, at the same time, Jake became distracted. He didn't bring any more presents. He didn't want to play fetch-the-porcupine. Even our walks were shorter than usual.

What was going on?

After dinner on Wednesday, I was dozing on the bed while Jake sat at his desk. He was supposed to be doing homework but instead he was staring at the wall, wiggling his leg, tapping his pencil and scratching his head. After a while he jumped up, went to the bathroom, came back and began to pace—three steps one way and three steps the other.

When I raised my head and woofed, he dropped his hindquarters down onto the bed next to me. "What am I going to do, Strudel? It's not even my fault. I never did one thing wrong, honest!"

This did not sound good. I leaned over and licked his hand.

Poor human. Tell me all about it.

"Anthony told me it was some errands," Jake said. "He said he'd pay me. I thought why not? Mom was after me to pay her back for the garden hose anyway."

Uh-oh.

"Besides," Jake went on, "I'm a little afraid of Anthony . . . and that big dog of his. Did you know he has a burn scar on his leg? Anthony, not the dog. He shows it off all the time so everyone knows how tough he is. He won't say how he got it."

I stretched out and got comfortable. This was sounding like it might be a long story.

"So anyway, the first time I worked for him, all I did was take an envelope to Richie at the doughnut shop. I had to be sure to give it to Richie, nobody else. Before that, I never met Richie. He goes to a different school. At the doughnut shop, I found him. He's kind of round and his job is cleaning up. I told him who I was, and he wanted to know if he could trust me, was I reliable?

"I said, 'Sure, I guess so.' And he grinned and said, 'Good man!' Then he opened the envelope, pulled out a five-dollar bill and gave it to me. 'Buy something for your girlfriend,' he said. 'You've got a girlfriend, right? Anthony says you're sweet on that girl Lisa.'

"That's a lie, Strudel. I'm not sweet on anybody. Lisa and I are friends is all.

"But Richie laughed like he'd made a hilarious joke. And besides, what did I care? I just got five dollars for walking two blocks!

"Now I wish I would've wondered about what was going on. Why was there cash in an envelope? How'd Richie and Anthony get that much money? But I didn't, because I liked having money in my pocket, Strudel. I liked buying stuff for you, too. Mom was too busy to ask about it. Only Mutanski did.

"Then last week Anthony asked me to do something different, something bad, something I would never ever do. When Anthony asked me, it must've showed on my face I was scared, 'cause he said, 'This is no big deal, punk. Even if you get caught—and you won't if you do what I tell you, but even if you do—you'll get off easy. Being just a little dude, you'll get nothing but a ride home from the cops.'

"I said, 'Okay, if it's no big deal, how come you can't do it?' And he said he and Richie have been in trouble before. The cops know them. If they got caught, it would be YSC for sure. That's what they call jail for kids around here, in case you didn't know.

"I tried to tell Anthony it wasn't just getting caught that worried me. It was also that I didn't want to do it. It's mean, Strudel. It's something so bad I don't even want to say.

"Finally I told him flat no. I told him I didn't have to. And you know what he said, Strudel? He said, 'You'll do it because I asked you to, and I asked very pleasantly, didn't I? No bad language. No threats. Nothing like that . . .'

"The way Anthony said it, I knew he meant it wouldn't be so pleasant if he had to ask again. And here's the thing, Strudel: He gave me a week, and the week is almost up."

Among dachshunds' many fine qualities is sensitivity, particularly to a human in distress. I felt terrible about what Jake was telling me, and more terrible because of my own predicament with the Pier 67 Gang. Just like Anthony was bullying Jake, Capo was bullying me.

Anyway, it's my dachshund sensitivity that accounts for the tummy upset I experienced that night. I won't be disgusting with the details. I'll just mention that yet another mess was left on Jake's rug.

You can guess the rest.

In spite of the weather, Mom decreed I had to spend the next day outside on the patio. I shivered when I heard this news. Best case, I would be cold, hungry and anxious all day. Worst case? I would be tormented by black-hearted feline visitors.

Eighteen

Jake left for school early. Mutanski carried me—wriggling and woofing in protest—toward the sliding glass doors.

You don't understand! Those cats are evil! The pigeons say they have no souls!

Mutanski held on tight. "Sorry, buddy." She grabbed an extra blanket as if that would protect me from feline claws. "You know Mom can't handle messes. Maybe Jake can get you a sweater with the next paycheck he gets from his life of crime. *Awwww*, wouldn't you look cute in a teensy little sweater of your own?"

I don't snarl at my own humans, but with that comment, Mutanski was pushing her luck.

Once the sliding doors had closed, I chased my tail to warm up. Then I made my usual circuit of my domain, took a drink of water and curled up on my cushion to wait. Anxious as I was, I must have dozed off. Humans who think dogs are lazy don't realize the hard work we do in our dreams. That day I was running after a rabbit when all of a sudden it transformed itself into a cat as large and vicious as Capo.

In my dream I growled, and I guess I did in real life, too, because I startled myself awake. Then, from much too nearby, I heard an ugly sound: cat laughter.

The Pier 67 Gang was back! And Capo himself, I now saw, lay eye-to-eye with me, blowing his rank, rot-scented breath into my face.

"My dear dog," he said in his low, creepy voice, "you must have done something very bad to be shut out on this cold day. Let me guess. Did you piddle on the rug?"

For courage, I thought of Chief. If he could take on bank robbers, I could take on cats—even soulless strays with hot, glowing eyes. "N-n-n-none of your beeswax," I said.

My smart comment caused Pepito and Lamar to hiss. Then, from the hedge, came an echoing chorus: *sssss.*

How many cats had Capo brought this time, I wondered? I didn't dare turn around to look. I had to keep my eye on the boss.

Capo swished his tail, and the hissing stopped. His gang was nothing if not obedient.

"I instructed Pepito to finish up that cheap dog food of yours," the big cat continued. "You really must demand improvement, dear dog. Do it for your own self-respect."

I should have kept quiet, but I was thinking of Jake and Anthony. If I wanted Jake to stand up to that bully, I should stand up to this one.

Summoning my last ounce of bravado, I said, "If your gang is hungry enough to eat dog food, I suppose I should be charitable. I was raised to be generous with those less fortunate."

Capo's eyes flashed red, but then he seemed to relent. "We eat your food because we can, not because we have to. It's our way of reminding you who really runs the show around here. And this is another." Capo unsheathed his claws and nodded at Lamar, who, quick as lightning, bit my behind!

Aieee!

The pain was awful, and my reflex was to fight back. I swung around to confront Lamar and found instead an overwhelming force—countless felines advancing toward me, brandishing their teeth and claws flashing, waving their tails in malicious, snake-like motion.

My heart jumped. This was it. They would shred me the way I shredded that garden hose. I closed my eyes to await the first painful piercing strike, but then—oh wonderful sound—came the *scrape* of Mrs. Rodino's window.

"Pipe down, you dog, or else I'll—*oh!*"

Looking down, she saw the nasty pack of marauding cats. Did she react with appropriate horror and disgust? No. She reacted like this: *"Awww,* poor kitty-kitties! Does ums need some wuv? I will be right down!"

Then with a *crack* the window closed.

I opened my eyes. The expression on Capo's face was unfamiliar. Could it be fear? "She can't get in here, can she?" he said.

"I don't know." I knew about the gate between our property and hers, but I had never seen anyone use it, and the hinges were rusty.

"If there's one thing I can't stand," Capo muttered, "it's a cat-loving lady. *Now hear this.*" His meow was like a siren. "We are advancing in a rearward direction! I want to see your tails, and I want to see them now! *Go! Go! Go! Go! GO!*"

Nineteen

Capo's tail had just disappeared into the hedge when the rusty gate began to squeak and rattle. I backed away, expecting Mrs. Rodino to burst through at any second. But Mrs. Rodino did not. Apparently the gate was stuck.

Footsteps. Muttering. The scrape of metal against stone. Then the top of Mrs. Rodino's head appeared. From the way it wobbled, I figured she was standing on a chair, and not a very steady chair, either.

"Hello, dog," she said. "What happened to all those sweet, sweet kitties? Don't tell me you scared them away."

I wanted to laugh, but, still shaky after my encounter with the gang, I managed only a woof.

Of course Mrs. Rodino misunderstood. Cat lovers always do. "Don't you pull that guard-dog stuff on me," she said. "From now on, I'll be looking out for those kitties. Love is all they need, that and a little cleaning up."

After Mrs. Rodino's head was gone, I finally got the peace and quiet I so desperately needed. First things first, I checked my food bowl. Perhaps a morsel or two had been left behind? But no. The cats had cleaned me out.

Mrs. Rodino had smelled like dust, hand lotion and bleach. With her gone and the cats, too, I detected a sharp, musky animal aroma that could only be one thing—a rat, probably the same one I had smelled some time before, but lurking closer now.

It seemed I was not alone.

Being a hound, I nosed around beneath the hedge for information. Soon I knew that this rat ate lots of different foods, including meat, that it had been hanging out here on the patio for a while, perhaps long enough to see the cats, that it was healthy and past middle age, that it did not have a mate or pups.

In other words, my company was an old bachelor rat. I had no sooner determined this than the rodent himself popped his head out of the leaves. It was gray and unevenly furred, with black beady eyes, scruffy faded-pink ears and nose, stiff whiskers and impressive yellow teeth.

"Hello, Strudel," he said. "I thought it best to greet you before you nosed me out. Some dogs dislike rats."

Some dogs included me. Rats reputedly resemble badgers— tough, grumpy and cunning. And, as you will remember, I was bred to hate badgers.

On the other hand, I had learned from my experience with Johanna to be wary of my own preconceptions. Also, it is usually worthwhile to be polite. So rather than biting his head off—literally—I said, "Hello, rat. You have the advantage of me. I do not know your name."

"I am Oscar," he said, "like the playwright, Oscar Wilde. I come from a long line of backstage rats. You've heard of Oscar Wilde, of course?"

"Oh yes," I lied. "The playwright Oscar Wilde. And where do you come from, Oscar?"

"Originally or just now?" the rat asked.

"Just now," I said.

"My country place. It's quite nearby. I was closing it up for winter. And you needn't worry that I have designs on your food the way the cats do. My tastes are more eclectic than theirs."

"So you know about the cats?" I said. "About their, uh . . . visits?"

This was very embarrassing. It's a sorry dog indeed that loses its food to cats. I hoped Oscar Wilde was not a blabbermouth like the pigeons.

"Those cats are a scourge," Oscar said firmly. "There's hardly a songbird or rodent left on the riverbank."

I didn't know what a *scourge* was, but the way the rat curled his lips implied it was bad. I felt reassured. And come to think of it, rats, like pigeons, are cats' natural enemies.

"Is it possible you would be willing to help me vanquish the gang?" I asked. "It's awful going hungry in the afternoons. It's awful being mauled."

"Yes, that bite looks bad," said Oscar. "But *vanquish* meaning just exactly what?"

I sighed and laid my head on my paws. "I'm not sure. I only know I want them out of my territory."

Oscar wiggled his whiskers. "And what makes this *your* territory?"

"It just is," I said. "I never thought about why, but I guess because the humans gave it to me."

Oscar cocked his head. "And what made it theirs to give?"

I opened my mouth and closed it again. This rat was a philosopher. His questions were hard to answer.

"The truth is," the rat went on, "we all of us share one big territory whether we want to or not. Are there ants here on the patio?"

"Oh yes." My snout itched with the memory.

"And worms? And beetles? And butterflies, birds and bees?"

"Sometimes. They are in and out."

"So who are you to say it's yours, or your humans' either? It belongs to all the creatures that use it. It has taken me most of my life to learn you can waste a lot of blood defending something that was never yours to begin with. Live and let live. We all of us have to learn to get along."

I said, "Oh," but what I meant was *Oh dear.* Philosophical or not, this added up to an excuse for refusing to help me deal with the cats.

But then Oscar uttered one word, an important one: "however."

"However?" I repeated eagerly.

With his hind leg Oscar scratched his ear, and for the first time I noticed that the leg was crooked and the ear torn. "There are limits to what a body can put up with— limits that begin when someone, like a cat, refuses to play by the rules."

Twenty

Oscar saw me look at his damaged leg and ear. "You're wondering what happened to me, aren't you?" he asked.

"Oh, no. Of course not. You look fine. Very handsome, in fact." I hoped I hadn't hurt his feelings.

Oscar chuckled, a deep chittering sound much nicer than the ugly screech of cats. "I know what I look like, Strudel. I am an old and battered rat. But old and battered is better than the alternative, wouldn't you say?"

I wasn't sure what he meant by that, but I agreed because I hoped he would tell his story.

"It was the Pier 67 Gang that did this to me," Oscar went on. "Back in the day, my clan lived in a theater near the waterfront. When it closed, supplies ran short, and we made the decision to migrate to a warehouse. There was plenty of food at first, but all that changed when the cats arrived."

"Where did they come from?" I asked.

"A human dumped a litter of kittens, which soon grew

into cats. Seeing strays around, more humans dumped more kittens. Once they had gobbled up the easy prey, they went after tougher, more challenging fare—in other words, us rats.

"Cats are cowardly creatures," Oscar said. "Only in desperation will they attack an animal that fights back. But eventually they got hungry enough to try it. Capo himself attacked me, and only with help from good fortune did I escape. Decimated, my clan broke up, and I've been on my own since then."

Oscar's story made me wonder whether it was only the losers who believed in sharing territory. The winners, after all, had what they wanted.

But then I thought again.

The winners still have to defend their gains against attack. If everyone agreed to share, there would be no winners and losers, and no need for bloody destruction either.

Oh my—the company of this rat was making me philosophical, too!

A familiar feathery smell intruded on my thoughts, and a moment later Johanna had landed on the patio in front of Oscar and me.

"Excuse me," she said. "Pigeons never eavesdrop, but I couldn't help overhearing, hearing what you were saying, you know. I believe you mentioned the Pier 67 Gang, that is, the gang of evil cats that lives at Pier 67?"

"Johanna, this is Oscar," I said. "Oscar, meet Johanna."

"I've seen you around, seen you many times, of course," the pigeon said politely.

"And I've seen you as well, but ordinarily"—Oscar looked at me—"pigeons and rats don't have a great deal to do with one another."

"We're up there, and they're down here. No call for us

to meet, no call at all," Johanna explained. "But now and then we make common cause against an enemy, that is to say the cats."

"Are you suggesting we join forces?" I asked hopefully.

"I am," said Johanna, "that is, am I?"

"Yes!" I said.

"I'm not sure I'm up to it," said Oscar. "These days, I am a meek, mild-mannered rat."

"We'll be right there with you," said Johanna, "wherever *there* turns out to be."

"Do you have a plan?" I asked her.

"A plan?" the pigeon repeated. "What part of 'birdbrain' don't you understand? We pigeons are good scouts, good flyers and good eaters. But we are not much for planning, not planners, we pigeons, not much."

Added to the strain of dealing with the Pier 67 Gang, the effort of talking to Johanna was exhausting. "Then how should we begin?" I asked.

"Oh, you'll think of something," cooed the pigeon, "think of something, I have faith. You see, I have personal reasons for hating the cats, hating the gang of strays, you know.

"I was a young mother with my first nest, living in an abandoned warehouse on Pier 67. Just as the cats attacked Oscar, they attacked the nest that my mate and I had constructed from twigs, attacked the nest and my mate, too, for he was guarding the eggs that day, two white and perfect eggs.

"They killed my mate and smashed the eggs, did this as I hovered above them, watching in horror, powerless to prevent the bloodshed. So many cats and claws and teeth, everywhere eggshell scattered, and the feathers of my love, his feathers and blood all mixed with the eggshell and twigs. It's a sight I wish I could forget but can't and never will."

The pigeons on the wire above Johanna cooed in commiseration. Poor bird, I thought. Seeing her nest destroyed and her mate murdered—why, it must have been like an *apocalypse* for her. No wonder she hated the cats. But here she was, she had come through.

"We pigeons," she said, "are optimists, natural born and raised. Somehow in the end we know we'll prevail, we'll triumph, we'll win, we'll fly."

"Rats are optimists, too," said Oscar. "We make the best of things and bounce back. It's partly positive attitude and partly good digestion."

By this time the sun was low in the sky. Mutanski would be home soon.

"Can we meet again tomorrow?" Johanna asked. "How 'bout if we meet tomorrow?"

"I can't tell if I'll be out here tomorrow," I explained. "It depends on the weather and the humans."

"We'll watch for you," said Oscar, "and for an opportunity to continue our conversation."

Twenty-One

That afternoon, I greeted Mutanski with extra enthusiasm. Teaming up with Oscar and Johanna made me feel better. Even though my allies did not exactly belong to species you'd take to the dog park and introduce around, I liked them. And I thought their skills would come in handy . . . just as soon as I figured out how.

Once again Mutanski played veterinarian on my wound.

"That boxwood hedge is vicious," she said. "This one almost looks like a bite."

It is! It is! It is! I told her. *But never mind that, come on, let's play!*

And that is what we did, chasing one way around the living room and back, until we heard Jake's key in the lock.

"See ya later, Strudel." Mutanski winked and headed to the kitchen to get herself a human treat. By now I understood she didn't want Jake to know she and I were friends. I didn't see why not.

Another human mystery to ponder.

Jake came in the door frowning, his head down, moving slowly.

Was he sick?

He needed a solid dose of doggie affection. I ran around his feet, jumped up to lick his fingers, scooted between his legs—played the clown and then some.

It didn't work.

"Not now, Strudel. Quit it, wouldja? Sheesh, you are a pain in the behind sometimes, you know that?"

I was stunned and hurt.

A few times my previous human had told me to "ratchet it down a notch" when I was an over-rambunctious puppy. But no one had ever called me a pain in the behind before. Not even Arnie.

Tail between my legs, I jumped up on the plaid chair in the living room, circled twice and laid myself down to wait out Jake's bad mood. In the meantime I closed my eyes, hoping to dream up a plan for vanquishing stray cats.

Jake was quiet at dinner and hardly touched the food on his plate. Eating with us as usual, Arnie just had to make a comment. "That's good spaghetti you're wasting there, pal," he said. "Don't you know there's plenty o' kids'd be glad to see that on their plates?"

"I am not your pal," said Jake.

Jake's mom stepped in. "Jake's tired, aren't you, honey? I'm sure he didn't mean—"

"I'm not that tired and I did, too, mean," Jake said.

Arnie dropped his fork. Even from my spot in the living room, I heard it go *clink* against his plate. "You are a rude, ungrateful and generally worthless—"

The legs of Jake's chair scraped the floor as he got up from the table in a hurry. "What are you even doing here?" Jake said. "You're not part of our family!"

Mom said, "Calm down! Everybody, just calm down!"

Mutanski put in, "Who set the loonies free?"

At the same time, the stomp of Arnie's big-booted feet told me he had stood up to go after Jake. "You get back here, you snot-nose!" he said. "I am an invited guest, and—"

Barking furiously, I was off the chair and on the floor in a heartbeat.

Dachsie to the rescue! Leave my human alone!

Arriving in the kitchen, I saw Jake turn to face Arnie, which caused Arnie, displaying trademark grace and poise, to step back . . . landing a big foot hard on yours truly.

Ow-owowowow!

Surprised to feel dog where floor should be, Arnie lost his balance and stumbled into Jake. Now they were both on the floor. I don't know if Jake and Arnie had intended to wrestle, but humans tangled up the way they were could hardly help it. Meanwhile, I took advantage of my short stature and scooted away to assess my wounds.

Bitten by a cat *and* stepped on! It had been a bad day for Strudel. Lucky I'm a dachshund, and dachshunds are tough as nails.

"Stop it this minute, you two!" yelled Mom. "Or so help me, you can *both* leave this house!"

"Oh, like threats are gonna help," Mutanski said, and, without further ado, she doused the wrestlers with a gallon of spaghetti water from the pot. "I'm only sorry it's cooled off," she said.

Gurgles, sputters, gasps, and finally Arnie's strangled cry: "I'm drowning!"

"No, you're not," Mom said, and tossed them each a

dish towel. "When you've wiped the water out of your eyes, Jake, you might as well mop the floor. As for you"—she looked at Arnie—"go on home and we'll talk tomorrow. If you're lucky."

"Can I at least get my dinner to go?" Arnie asked.

Mom's answer was to glare.

It was quiet after Arnie left, as if, without having to say a word, Jake, Mom and Mutanski had come to an agreement: They'd been through more than enough drama for one evening. If Mom was mad at Jake, or Jake at Mom, or Mutanski at everybody—all that could wait. Now it was time for no-fuss eating, cleaning up and cooperating. Jake even did the mopping without being reminded.

At bedtime he asked me if I wanted him to read some Chief. "I think it might be a good distraction," he said. "I can't go to bed yet anyway."

Distraction from what, I wondered? And why couldn't he go to bed? It was almost time, anyway, and I for one was exhausted.

"Where were we?" Jake said. "Chapter Seven, right? It's called 'Cattle Rustlers.'"

Chief, Dog of the Old West

On a hot, dusty day in Groovers Gulch, Sheriff Silver was sitting at the desk in the sheriff's office, his faithful dog, Chief, napping by his side. Suddenly Chief, who was sleek and powerfully built, sat up straight, rotated his ears and barked the sharp bark that meant: danger!

"What is it, Chief?" Sheriff Silver asked, but already the canine had scrambled to his feet and trotted to the door. Soon the two were standing on the wooden walk that ran the length of Main Street. Only

then did the sheriff's inferior human ears sense the sound that had disturbed Chief. It was a rumble like distant thunder, and it was growing louder. At the same time, a brown cloud of powdery dust billowed on the horizon north of town.

Sheriff Silver knew what that was.

So did Chief.

And so did the leading townsfolk, now gathering in the blazing sunshine on the treeless street.

"Stampede!" cried Sheriff Silver.

"A-yup," said one of the townsfolk.

Dog and sheriff regarded each other with alarm: The old home place lay north of town . . . dead in the path of the cattle stampede!

"Head 'em up, boy!" cried Sheriff Silver as he grabbed the reins of his palomino, swung his lean body into the saddle and galloped toward home.

Chief streaked ahead like a well-aimed bullet.

Our heroes were moving fast, but the raging herd of beef on the hoof had a big head start. Sheriff Silver didn't want to think about what would happen if the bovines reached the home place first.

That was the end of the chapter. Jake turned the page but did not read on. I couldn't believe it. Would Chef Pierre and Rachel Mae be all right? Or would they be flattened by cows?

Woof, I said, but my human was staring into space. I licked his hand, which tasted like spaghetti.

"What? Oh . . . sorry, Stru," Jake said. "I got a lot on my mind. See, if I'm gonna do it, tonight's the—"

Before he could finish the sentence, his mom called, "Bedtime, Jake! And don't forget to brush your teeth!"

Jake didn't answer right away. Finally he sighed. "Mom?" he called back. "Uh, sorry, but I forgot to walk Strudel."

A walk? A walk? A walk? Yippeee!

I was on the floor and down the stairs before Jake even put on his shoes. I heard him say something to his mom, and I heard his mom reply. I could guess what she was saying: "Come right back, and be careful."

Twenty-Two

Outside, the pavement felt slick beneath my paws and the air held the damp promise of snow. Cold weather dulls the smellscape, but I still picked up greetings from Rudy and Luca at the power pole, then left replies of my own. Rudy had visited only a few minutes before. It must have been Lisa's dad who walked him. Lisa was never allowed out this late.

When Jake and I reached the end of the block, I was cold and ready to turn back. I thought of my warm and cozy bed, glad to have a home on a night like this. Then Jake surprised me by tugging to the left. He wasn't gentle about it either.

"Come on, Stru, we don't have all night, you know. Stop that stupid sniffing. We gotta hurry."

Stupid sniffing? But this is my walk! Where are we going, anyway?

Wherever it was, it was far, far away—a much longer walk than I was used to, especially on a school night. Mom was going to be awfully annoyed, if she was even awake.

Few people were out on the street. Light and music streamed from bars and pizza places, but most businesses were closed, and most houses quiet. Still there was always an assortment of smells—delicious, disgusting and neutral. Combined, they made up the aroma symphony that defined the neighborhood.

There were also new dogs to identify, but when I tried to stop and inhale the details, Jake pulled me along with a jerk. Where were we going, anyway? Why were we out so late?

At last we arrived at a block I knew. Jake's grandpa's bakery was here. Mom had brought me once in the car. Even now when the bakery was closed, I recognized the smell of the cannoli—sweet cheese, orange peel and cooking grease.

For some reason, Jake and I walked back and forth along this block twice. Finally he muttered, "I guess it's now or never," and we crossed the street. Midway along the next block he stopped, looped my leash around a tree and whispered hoarsely, "Stay, Strudel. I'll be back."

Stay? Whaddaya mean, stay? You're my human! You can't leave me!

Only now, as Jake walked away, did I notice he was wearing his backpack. This was strange. He only wore his backpack for school. I watched as he swung it off his shoulders, pulled out a baseball cap and tugged it down on his head. Then he pulled out something else, and put the pack back on. A moment later, he walked under a streetlight and I saw what he was carrying.

It was a brick.

This whole operation gave me the willies, so I sat back on my haunches and howled. I didn't like being left by myself! I didn't like this neighborhood! And I didn't like the cold! I would have howled some more, too, but then Jake turned around. Even from a distance, I could see how angry he was, angry enough that I closed my mouth and kept quiet.

Jake recrossed the street and stopped on the corner in front of a store we had passed. It was a mini-mart, by the smell of it—tobacco, salt, chewing gum and plastic. The store had a big glass window. Fascinated and scared, I watched my human raise the brick in front of him, swing it around behind and pitch it forward with frightening force.

Crack—the night was split by the awful sound of glass shattering.

I couldn't help it, I yelped. The next sound was the *slap-slap-slap* of Jake's shoes running toward me on the pavement. By the time he reached me, his eyes were wide and his face tear-streaked. I could smell the fear in his sweat.

"Strudel." He exhaled my name, and in a single quick motion unlooped the leash from the tree.

After that the two of us ran as we had never run before.

The breaking glass had been so loud, I expected a consequence—shouting, a police siren, *something.* But the reality was a quiet in which our breathing was the only sound. One by one, the blocks unspooled—sidewalk, street, sidewalk, street.

My chest hurt. I stepped on something sharp. Jake stumbled on broken pavement. It started to snow. We kept running.

Every thought left my head except the need to put two paws in front of two others. Only when we reached the familiar smellscape of our own neighborhood did my brain start to work: My human was going to be in big trouble!

A block before our house, Jake slowed to a walk. I didn't

notice, and ran right past till the end of the leash pulled me back with a jerk.

"Oh, sorry, Stru." Jake's voice was kind now, back to normal. Instantly, I forgave him everything. Loyalty is in a dachshund's blood.

"We have to be super quiet, Stru, okay?" Jake whispered as we approached the steps.

I wagged my tail and raised my nose. Come what might, I would stay by my human's side.

The rattle of Jake's key in the lock seemed as loud as an alarm. I flinched, half expecting Colonel Joshua Trueheart and the 11th Cavalry to be waiting for us in the living room.

But when the door opened, the house was dark and still. Jake pushed the door closed and locked it. He scraped his shoes on the mat and brushed the damp snow off his coat. I shook myself dry. Then the two of us tiptoed up the stairs, the only sound now the jangling of the tags on my collar. In Jake's bedroom, he collapsed on his bed and pulled me close. I could feel his heart beating fast against his ribs.

For a moment we were silent, still waiting for something bad to happen—a light to go on, Mom's voice to call out. When it didn't, Jake whispered in my ear, "I don't care how Anthony threatens me, Strudel. I will never do anything like that again."

Twenty-Three

The next day was Friday. Mom, Mutanski and Jake got up, got dressed, ate cereal and put on coats. They were in a hurry as always. No one in that house had time to say much on weekday mornings.

I think I was the only one who noticed that Jake was paler than usual, and he threw most of his cereal down the sink. He was also strangely polite. Mutanski made a comment about how he'd forgotten to walk me till late, how he still wasn't responsible enough for a dog.

Instead of snapping at her, he said, "Maybe you're right."

Outside there was a dusting of snow, and it was plenty cold. I wouldn't be out on the patio that day. I wondered when I would I have a chance to meet with Oscar and Johanna, when we could come up with a plan of attack.

The Pier 67 Gang was living on borrowed time. They just didn't know it yet.

That evening Grandpa brought pizza as usual. Unfortunately, Arnie also came over. The way Mom explained it to Mutanski after school, Arnie had texted her at work, a big "I'M SORRY! I ACTED LIKE A DOPE!" complete with hearts and sad faces.

Then he had asked to come to dinner and promised to be on his best behavior—even knowing Grandpa would be there, too.

"It'll be okay," Mom told Mutanski. "I think he means it this time. I think he's learning to control his temper."

Mutanski rolled her eyes.

At dinner, I took my place beneath Jake's chair. If I could take on the Pier 67 Gang, I ought to be able to handle Arnie. Besides, only under Jake's chair could I expect my weekly bites of dropped pizza sausage.

At first, the human conversation was uninteresting. Arnie, Grandpa and Jake all agreed that the refs had stolen the game from the Eagles the Sunday before. Grandpa said the Frogs' costumes for the Mummers Parade on New Year's Day would be better than ever this year.

"My dad was a Mummer, and my uncle, too," Arnie said, "but I never could see it for myself. All that practice just so you can party New Year's Eve and parade in a costume on New Year's Day?"

"It's a lot of fun," Grandpa said. "The guys are some'a my best friends, and it's tradition. Mumming goes back hundreds of years—to before the United States even got started."

"It does?" Jake said.

"*Duh,*" Mutanski said.

Grandpa laughed. "A long time ago, a lot of people in

European towns celebrated the winter holidays by mumming—putting on masks and costumes, then going out to visit the neighbors and drink a little punch, too. Immigrants brought those customs to Philadelphia in the 1600s, but then the Quakers took over, and they weren't big partiers. On and off over the years mumming got outlawed, but eventually the tradition evolved into brigades parading like we have now."

"I never really got the 'brigade' thing," Mutanski said.

"A brigade is a social club, more or less," said Mom.

"*Duh,*" said Jake.

"Lots of emphasis on *social,*" said Grandpa. "The party on 2 Street at New Year's seems to last for days."

"I wish it was a little quieter," said Mom. "When there're firecrackers, it gets pretty darned loud."

"That's part of the tradition," Grandpa said. "Back in the day, they shot muskets. Anyway, there's no real damage done. Hey—that reminds me. Did you hear what happened to Betty?"

Jake made a choked sound in his throat, and my ears perked up.

"Of course I heard," said Mom. "South Philly's a small town, right? Somebody smashed the plate glass window at the Quik-Stop. Guess they'll never catch the guy."

"Probably not," said Grandpa. "Cops found the brick, but you seen one brick, you seen 'em all. Just kids, I guess. Still, Betty was pretty upset. Her store means a lot to her. She keeps it nice, and now it'll be boarded up till she can afford to get the window fixed."

"I never liked that woman," Arnie said.

There was a pause, then Grandpa asked, "And just why not?"

Mom spoke up. "Uh, Arnie? My dad and Mrs. Rossi . . . they're kind of an item."

Arnie said, "Is that a fact? My apologies, Mr. Allegro. She and I had some business dealings is all, and I never found her very cooperative."

"Still, she didn't deserve to have her window broken," Mom said.

"Kids today," said Arnie. "What're ya gonna do?"

Jake didn't talk to me that night before bed, or read me a Chief story either. Instead he cried into his pillow, but his sobs were silent, and neither Mom nor Mutanski heard. Thinking of Maisie—how her sympathy had helped me get through the tough times—I licked the tears off his ear.

The weather stayed cold, and Jake stayed pale. Mom kept asking if he felt okay, and he kept saying, "Yeah, Mom, I'm fine." I think he and I were both waiting for the police to connect him to the brick they found in Mrs. Rossi's store and show up at the front door to arrest him, but they didn't, and the only person who asked about Thursday was Mutanski. On Sunday afternoon she said, "Hey, little bro. You mighta fooled Mom, but I heard you come in Thursday night. It was almost midnight. What was up with that?"

We were in the living room, Jake and me on the sofa, Mutanski in the plaid chair doing homework. Had she made the connection between our walk and the broken window? "I'm sorry if I woke you," Jake said, still being strangely polite.

"You didn't, and that's not the point. Are you still mixed up with that Anthony kid, Arnie's nephew?"

"No," Jake said quickly. "I mean, not really."

"Okay," Mutanski said. "'Cause if you're ever tempted to be, I think I should explain something to you. Bad kids like to get help from good kids."

"What do you mean?"

"I mean, blockhead, that grown-ups think good kids don't do bad things. So if a bad kid can get a good one to do his dirty work, it helps him stay out of trouble."

Jake said, "Okay," and then it was quiet for a minute. I don't know about Jake's, but my heart was bumping along faster than usual. "Uh . . . Mutanski?" he finally said. "Was there a particular bad thing you were, uh . . . thinking of?"

"I knew it!" Mutanski pounced. "You did do something!"

"I never said—"

"What did you do?"

"Nothing," Jake said. "I didn't do anything."

For several seconds after that Mutanski looked at her brother, and her brother fidgeted.

Finally Mutanski shrugged. "If you say so," she said, and then she went back to her homework.

Twenty-Four

The next week was Thanksgiving. Unlike Halloween, this was a holiday I knew about. Ordinarily my previous human did not cook much, but every Thanksgiving morning he made something he called a casserole using green beans, mushrooms and fried onions from a can. In the afternoon, he would leave to visit some friends and take the casserole with him. Later he would come back with the empty dish, but more importantly with a foil container for me. In it was cooked turkey, potatoes and red stuff.

I loved the turkey and potatoes, but the red stuff was sour and terrible. I ate it anyway. I didn't want to hurt my human's feelings.

Since almost everything about this house was different from that one, I was surprised to learn my new humans also ate casserole, turkey and red stuff on Thanksgiving. I know because I got bites of each.

On Thanksgiving morning, Mom cooked while Jake

and Mutanski cleaned the house. Still being extra polite, Jake didn't complain about having to clean.

In the afternoon Grandpa came over with a pumpkin pie, and they all sat down to eat dinner. Arnie had what Mom called "other obligations."

"What's Betty Rossi doing for the holiday, Dad?" Mom asked. "You could've invited her here."

"She's laid up with a cold," Grandpa said. "I think she's flat exhausted. First there was the window. Then the kid who sweeps and stocks shelves for her quit. I told her I'd go over tomorrow and help out."

For some moments after that the only sounds were forks on plates, chewing and happy *mphs* of satisfaction. Then Jake said, "I could maybe help Mrs. Rossi out, too."

"Cripes," said Mutanski. "What is *wrong* with you, Jake? You've been nice for, like, a week now."

"I'm not being nice," Jake said.

"Yeah you are. It's annoying," said Mutanski.

"Here's an idea, Laura," Mom said. "You could be nice, too."

"Ha!" said Mutanski. "Not gonna happen."

"Give your brother some credit," Grandpa said. "Maybe he's just growing up. Sure, Jake, that would be great if you helped her out. We can talk more tomorrow."

After dinner, Grandpa, Mom and Jake turned on the TV while Mutanski cleaned up the kitchen. "Now who's being nice?" Jake asked.

"Not me," Mutanski said. "I just think anything's better than watching football."

Jake never told me about helping Mrs. Rossi at her store, but it must have gone pretty well. His sweat stopped smelling so nervous after that. His color came back. He was rude to Mutanski again.

Soon it was December, and it seemed as if the weather would be cold and gray till spring. How did Oscar and Johanna like the winter, I wondered? I wished we could finish making our plans.

On the other hand, I really really like being warm, comfortable and well-fed.

One day when Jake came home from school, I noticed that smell of fear again. What he told me that night explained why.

"Anthony's started up with me, Strudel," Jake said as he lay on top of his covers, staring at the ceiling. It wasn't quite bedtime yet. He hadn't even taken off his shoes. I was beside him in the crook of his arm. "He and Richie have a new assignment for me," he said. "That's what he called it, 'an assignment,' like it was homework or something.

"I told him I was kind of busy, and he grabbed the neck of my T-shirt. He didn't hurt me; he let go right away. He even smiled, which was almost the worst part because I got the point, Strudel. He's bigger than me. And stronger. And braver. Not to mention he has Luca . . . and tough as you are, Stru, you are no match for Luca."

In the tight space, I wiggled my tail as best I could.

Ha-ha-ha-ha-ha! That's what you think! Let me at him!

"I don't know what's gonna happen, Stru," Jake went on. "It seems like not that long ago, everything was great. I got you—my very own dog at last! All that reading we did helped me out in school, and I got to be friends with Lisa, too.

"Even working for Anthony and Richie was good at first. I had money of my own. But now that's all turned terrible, and I don't know what to do."

Jake's armpit smelled like boy sweat, meat loaf and mustard—delicious, in other words. I leaned over and gave him a smooch on the mouth for comfort. He said, "*Yuck, Strudel!*" and wiped off my slobber, but I knew he didn't really mind.

"Homework done?" Mom was in the doorway. "And what are you doing with your shoes on the bed, Mister?"

"It's done." Jake swung his feet over the side and sat up. "Sorry."

Mom frowned. "Sweetie? Have you been crying?"

Jake wiped his face with the back of his hand. "No, of course not, Mom. Strudel just licked me is all."

"Well, okay, if you say so." Mom didn't sound convinced. "How about if I let you stay up a little late if you want to? I bet Strudel could use a story."

I could! I could! I could! For all we know, the old home place has been stomped flat as a pancake!

Chief, Dog of the Old West

The palomino's powerful legs moved like steam-powered pistons beneath his sleek and shining coat. Two miles outside of town, the sheriff came over a rise and saw the home place spread out in the valley below, an idyllic picture postcard on the scrubby brown expanse of rock, desert and cactus.

The sheriff saw something else, too—the cause of the stampede. It was not spontaneous as he had surmised. Rather, the cattle had been spooked by rustlers who, even now, were whooping and hollering alongside, goading the herd on.

"Well I'll be dadblamed," said the sheriff. "What do you make of that, Chief? Uh, Chief?" Sheriff Silver

looked around and saw he now had an additional problem. His faithful dog was gone!

"Tarnation!" he cried, and then, "Giddyap, Ranger! Looks like we'll have to save the day without him."

Unbeknownst to Sheriff Silver, Chief had taken a shortcut through the sagebrush—a shortcut that put him directly in the path of the stampede. Now, choking on dust, he raced toward the southeasternmost hoof of the southeasternmost cow on the southeasternmost edge of the mass of rampaging beef.

The cow in question already had had a bad day, and this mutt was all she needed. Calling on unaccustomed agility, she do-si-doed to avoid his incisors, forcing the other cows to follow her lead.

Thus did Chief redirect the stampede to a course that missed the old home place entirely, except for a single zinnia whose stem was slashed by the hoof of a marginal heifer.

Sheriff Silver arrived at the house in time to see the stampede thunder past. When Chef Pierre and Rachel Mae realized how narrow had been their escape, they turned paper-pale and quivered like aspen leaves in a breeze.

"Sacre bleu!" cried Chef Pierre.

"I want revenge," said Rachel Mae, "in the name of my decapitated zinnia."

This was the end of the chapter, and ordinarily Jake would have closed the book. But both of us were eager to know what happened next.

Would Sheriff Silver get revenge?

"Let's keep reading, Strudel," Jake whispered. "Maybe if we're quiet, Mom won't hear."

When at last Chief straggled home, Sheriff Silver was waiting at the gate. "Where have you been? I was worried sick! Do you know the Gingham Gang provoked that stampede? And now—heaven help us—Rachel Mae is devising a plan to bring them to justice. Those black-hearted outlaws have disturbed the peace one time too many. Lookie here what they did to this zinnia!"

Chief was sorry about the zinnia, but after a day spent chasing cows, he was too tired to do any thinking that night. Instead he gulped some water, ate an ounce of leftover pâté, circled three times, lay down and fell deeply asleep.

As was his wont, the big red rooster crowed shortly before sunrise.

Sheriff Silver sat up in bed. "I hate that bird," he said. "I wish I could shut him up in the chicken coop for good."

Shut him up in the chicken coop for good? That phrase got Chief to thinking, and quick as anything, he was on his feet and whining at the door.

Sheriff Silver observed his dog's eagerness. "Just let me affix my spurs and silver star," he said, "for I see you are a dog on a mission."

The sun had just begun to paint the horizon when the sheriff, riding his palomino, commenced to follow Chief across the prairie. Their goal was Rockabox Canyon, location of the Gingham Gang's hideout, a place no townsperson dared venture for fear of being greeted with a hail of gunfire.

Before noon, man, dog and horse arrived at Strawberry Ice Cream Spire, a striking rock formation that stood on the rim of the canyon, marking its only *entrance. Early settlers had named the spire in honor of its pink boulders, which resembled giant scoops of ice cream.*

Sheriff Silver shook his head. "I never realized till now how unstable that thing is. Why, one good push and it would topple right into the canyon!"

Chief had been thinking the same thing. Now, without further ado, he fetched a baseball-sized rock, brought it to the sheriff and dropped it at his feet.

The sheriff was puzzled. "We have miscreants to catch, Chief. Is this really the right time to play?"

Woof, said Chief.

"Well, all right." The sheriff shrugged. "I guess we can spare a moment for recreation." Sheriff Silver went into his windup and zinged a fastball or, more accurately, a fast rock. As luck would have it—and as Chief intended—the rock hit Strawberry Ice Cream Spire square in its midsection, dislodging three critical pebbles.

For a long moment, nothing happened. Then from deep in the depths of the now teetering formation came the sound of an ominous rumble.

"Oops," said Sheriff Silver. "So much for recreation."

Blam-kablam-boomety-pow-crash-crash-crash! A hundred tons of strawberry-colored boulders spilled, slid and careened into the canyon below.

When at last the cloud of strawberry dust had settled, Sheriff Silver and Chief peered over the canyon rim. Just as Chief had anticipated, the rockslide had blocked the canyon's lone egress.

The Gingham Gang was trapped!

Not wishing to expire of hunger and thirst, the gang soon waved the white flag of surrender. Later *that day, leading townsfolk cleared the obstruction using a few deftly placed sticks of dynamite. After that, they trotted the Gingham Gang off to jail.*

Once again, Chief had prevailed over evil, and peace and justice had triumphed.

Jake closed the book and turned the light off. Then he rolled over and scratched me behind the ears.

"Reading makes me feel better, Strudel," he said. "I only wish real life was like that. I wish I could trap Anthony and Richie with a rockslide so they'd stop bothering me."

I wished my human could do that, too, but I didn't see how it would work exactly.

As for my own predicament with dirty rotten bad guys—*cats,* I mean—the Chief story had given me an idea.

Twenty-Five

When I trotted downstairs the next morning, Mom had the weather report on TV: clear and unseasonably warm, temperatures in the low 60s.

"That's good news for you, Strudel." Mom poured kibble into my dish. "You can spend the day outside in the sunshine. I wish I could do the same. Instead I'll be inside inhaling cleanser fumes."

As usual, it was Mutanski who put me out on the patio. Her goodbye was a two-handed rubdown from base of tail to collar. *Awwww,* it felt wonderful.

I love, love, love, love, love you, Mutanski!

"See you after school," she said.

Once Mutanski was gone, I made my usual rounds. The pigeons were roosting elsewhere. The ants had retreated deep underground for winter. The smell of rat was faint. Had Oscar gone underground, too?

I curled up on my pillow and made some refinements

to the plan the Chief story had inspired. Would it work? It would have to. It was the only plan I had.

Excited as I was, I must have dozed off. We dogs are very good at dozing. Finally a rustling in the hedge made me jump, and all at once my stomach clenched.

Had the gang returned?

But when I got a good whiff I relaxed.

"Wake up, canine!" Oscar's beady eyes peered over the pillow at me. "Rise and shine! Like all your kind, you are a lazy bum."

The rat was teasing me, and I teased back. "You're just envious," I said. "You spend your whole day grubbing for food, and still you can't be sure of what you'll find."

"Variety is the spice of life," said Oscar, "and besides, you can't be sure of your next meal either, not when you're paying tribute to the cats."

"That won't be for much longer," I said. "I have devised a plan."

Oscar fidgeted with his whiskers. "Do tell. And is there a part for me in this plan?"

"For you and for a pigeon," I said. "You don't even have to audition."

Nervously Oscar swiped a paw over his damaged ear. "You remember that I am a meek, mild-mannered rat?" he said.

"I do remember, and I promise you won't have to confront any cats directly. Your job is more behind-the-scenes."

"In that case, I am willing to discuss it," said Oscar, and at the same time we heard the fluttering of wings.

"Not to worry! Don't worry!" cooed Johanna, gliding to rest on the bench. "What can I do for you, Strudel? Have you made a plan? Isn't this a glorious sunny day, though? How I love the sun! Have you made the plan in question?"

"I have," I said, and with that I laid out my plan in detail, with itemized action items numbered one through six.

"That's it?" Oscar said when I was done. "That's the whole thing?"

"What's the matter with it?" I asked, a little hurt.

"I just expected something a bit more, uh . . . complex," said Oscar.

Johanna, in contrast, showed her enthusiasm by marching in place and bobbing her head. "Elegance is often simple and simplicity often elegant. Do you follow? Follow me!"

Apparently unconvinced, Oscar cleared his throat. "I have another observation, if you will. This plan relies too much on the behavior of humans. In my experience, it's always risky to count on them."

Johanna disagreed. "We city animals all count on humans," she said. "It's humans that created the city. It's humans that provide us most of our food and our shelter, our shelter and our food, that is. And of us three, who knows humans best? Who has studied them most closely? Strudel, that's who. I say we count on him."

"Well, ye-e-es," the rat said thoughtfully. "And additionally, it's true that the dog's idea does take advantage of Capo's Achilles' heel."

"Achilles? Who is this Achilles? I don't believe we're acquainted," Johanna said.

"I know him only by reputation myself," said Oscar. "He was a human warrior dipped as a baby in a magic river. The magic protected him from injury. But there was a problem. When his mother dipped him, she held him by one heel, so that heel was unprotected. It was his only weak spot."

"His mother should have flipped him over and dunked his feet," I said.

"Agreed," said Oscar, "but if she had we would lack the useful and poetic expression 'Achilles' heel.' In any event, Capo's Achilles' heel is his rotundity, his too-well-rounded shape, I mean—oh dear, Johanna! Listen to me! Now I'm talking like you."

Johanna chuckled, a pleasant sound that combined coo, tweet and burble. "It happens. I've heard it happen," she said. "Now when do we implement Strudel's plan? Carry it out, I mean? I believe I can expect some help from the flock. The flock will help us, won't you?"

The answering coos from above said yes.

Like her speech patterns, Johanna's confidence must have been contagious, because now Oscar got over his hesitation. "The warm weather won't last," he said. "If we don't act soon, we'll have to wait for spring. I say we act the next time the gang pays a visit. Even today, if need be."

"So soon?" I said, knowing there would be no going back once Johanna and Oscar got to work.

"I can get started right away," Oscar said. "I had a generous helping of rotten meatballs from the alley for breakfast. I won't need to scavenge again before lunchtime. Are you ready, Johanna? Is the flock ready?"

"Ready as we'll ever be," she said. "All for one, and one for Strudel!"

Twenty-Six

I had expected to have time to refine my plan further, or at least to give myself a final pep talk. But once the rat and the pigeon got going, everything moved fast. The sun had just peaked in the sky when Johanna and Oscar returned to tell me Parts One and Two were complete.

"Already?" I said. "I mean, I mean, I mean—that's great."

Oscar wiggled his whiskers and blinked his beady eyes. "The next part is up to you, Strudel. I hope you know what you've gotten yourself into."

"I'll be looking out for you, looking out," said Johanna, "but from a safe distance away, safe and safely away, you might say. Having seen them in action, I have healthy respect for the weaponry of felines, their teeth and claws, that is."

This reminder of the Pier 67 Gang's viciousness made my old scars burn. I might have lost heart right then, but I remembered Chief. He had caught a gang of cattle rustlers in a box canyon. Surely I could catch a stray cat on the patio.

"Where did you stash the nesting materials?" I asked.

"Just the other side of the fence." Oscar pointed with the tip of his tail. "Under an outcropping of ivy."

I started to ask how much they had collected. Were they sure it was enough? But I did not get the chance. From the power lines above us came the sound of the pigeon alarm. "Cats coming! Cats coming! Gang spotted at the head of the alley!"

Johanna hopped and fluttered into the air. "Good luck, Strudel! We'll work as fast as we can."

Forepaw to ear, Oscar gave a quick salute. "Curtain going up, canine! All eyes on you."

I barely had time to turn around before feline stench filled my nostrils. It was ranker than usual that day. The cats must have been hungry enough to go Dumpster diving, something they usually considered beneath their dignity.

"My dear dog, how pleasant it is to see you again." Capo emerged from the gap in the hedge. Over the fence came Pepito, Lamar and four cats I hadn't seen before. These last cats posted themselves at the four corners of the patio as sentries.

One of the four, a black cat with a white nose and throat, was dangerously close to Johanna and Oscar's current operation on the other side of the fence. What if he heard them? What if he sounded the alarm?

My plan would fail. The cats would win. I thought of what Johanna told me they'd done to her nest and her mate. This time it might not only be a few gashes in my flesh and humiliation. This time their revenge might be something much worse. It might even be deadly.

I couldn't think of that now, though. If I did, I would lose heart, and I had a part to play.

"G-g-g-good afternoon, Capo." My stammer wasn't an act. It was for real. My heart was racing.

"We've just come by for a snack," Capo said, "and perhaps to take a short rest. You have such a sunny spot here, and your pillow is just right. It's kind of you to extend your hospitality."

Pepito, as frail and dirty as ever, was already leaning into my food dish. Much as I hated the cats, this one's appearance was so pathetic I almost felt sympathy. As for Capo, he seemed to feel nothing at all. Pepito had barely sniffed the food when the boss cat cuffed him across the face and knocked him out of the way.

Now Pepito's dirty nose sported a line of bright red blood.

"It's not your turn," Capo told the white cat in his oily purr. "It's my turn."

Capo, big belly brushing the ground, waddled over to my food dish, leaned down and ate one bite after another, chewing each with exaggerated thoroughness as Pepito watched miserably. What had he done to displease the boss? Was Capo simply reminding his gang who was in charge? Or perhaps cruelty was just the way he amused himself.

"Anyone else care for a morsel?" Capo asked at last. "Marco? Fritz? Lamar?" The other cats looked away or washed their faces. "Oh, all right, Pepito. I suppose you may have what's left. But do be careful with portion size. I wouldn't want you to get fat."

Capo laughed at his own joke, and the other cats laughed, too. It would have been dangerous not to.

Without so much as a mew, Pepito slunk over to my food bowl and ate the few remaining bites.

All this time, my ears had been tuned for the sounds of rat and pigeons at work. They were executing the riskiest part of my plan—Part Three.

Part One had been to assess the size of the hole in the

fence, the one through which Capo entered and exited. Part Two was to gather enough twigs and other nesting materials to plug the hole up tight. Part Three was to do the job. My allies were working from the back side of the fence, the alley side. But any telltale noise might tip off the gang.

The city's background noises—sirens, car horns, trucks, shouting, jets and helicopters—had so far covered the sounds of rat and pigeons at work, and the black-and-white sentry nearest the hole in the fence had not once looked concerned.

The other risk was that the cats would decide to leave before Part Three was concluded. This was my department. I had to keep them here—distract them—but conversation is surprisingly difficult when you're terrified. With nothing to say, I stared dumbly at the boss cat as he meticulously groomed his claws.

"What are you looking at, my dear dog?" Capo asked me at last.

"Y-y-you," I answered truthfully. "Uh . . . so tell me, Capo, how are things down by the river these days? Good? I mean, I hope they're good. I hope all of you are eating well?"

If Capo was surprised by my concern, he didn't show it. "Times were better before there were so many of us," he admitted. "I don't mind telling you it's a lot for one cat to oversee. Happily, we have this secluded paradise to return to anytime we're hungry." He laughed his ugly feline laugh. "In the never-ending conflict between our two species, my dear dog, it is good to know we cats have absolute dominion in this pleasant little corner."

This was too much. Reflexively, I raised my hackles and growled. It was a low, soft sound, but Capo heard it anyway, and his eyes flashed. "Watch yourself, my dear dog," he said smoothly, "or I'll shred your hide like mozzarella cheese."

Much as my hound-dog nature longed to attack, I managed to hold it back. It would be foolish to get into a fight now that my plan was so close to completion.

At least I hoped it was. In essence, the pigeons and Oscar were building a super-sturdy nest in the hole in the fence. Nesting was something they were good at. But, being small, they had to transport the materials—twigs, leaves, dried grasses, feathers, paper and other small items of litter—one at a time to lay them in place.

I hoped they were working fast. I hoped Johanna had managed to recruit a lot of volunteers. I wished I had asked them how long the job would take. Not being a nest builder myself, I had no idea. Were they almost done? Halfway done?

"So, Capo, I'm, uh . . . surprised you guys like dog food so much," I said. "Or do you like dog food? How does it compare to cat food? I never ate cat food myself." I didn't add what I was thinking, that the very thought gave me indigestion.

"My dear dog, we strays are adaptable creatures. We have to be," said Capo. "It's true I prefer my food to be fresh, still wiggling if possible. Dog food tastes like cinders and waste, but at least it never tries to escape."

Now the cat was insulting my food! I vowed to remain calm. I even asked a couple more questions, all the time keeping one eye on the black-and-white sentry.

Capo was schooling me on the flavor variations in mackerel when the sentry lifted his head. "Excuse me, boss? I hear some kinda activity goin' on out back in the alley."

Capo turned to look at the sentry, which was fortunate. Otherwise he might've seen my panicked expression.

"What kind of activity?" Capo asked.

"Rodents, maybe. How would I know?" said the sentry. "It ain't like I got X-ray vision or something."

Capo blinked. "Dominic? You are a son of mine, but I don't like your attitude."

The sentry shifted his haunches and swished his tail. "Yeah? Well there's times I don't like yours either, Dad."

Capo turned to the black cat with the sharp claws. "Lamar, would you mind taking care of my son for me? I'm so comfortable just now on the dog's pillow."

"Hey, wait a sec—" the sentry started to say, but his words dissolved in a howl of pain. Lamar had sighted and pounced, overwhelming the young cat in a blur of teeth and claws. The punishment, loud and ferocious, lasted only a few seconds.

"That will do," Capo said. "And let that be a lesson to the rest of you."

The sentry, Dominic, was left hunched over, panting and defeated. Both his ears were torn; his blood dotted the ground around him. I couldn't help but stare, and when I did I saw him look up and give Capo a look of sheer hatred.

Capo didn't seem to notice. Instead he said to no cat in particular, "I think we've imposed on the canine long enough. But we'll see you again soon, my dear dog. Till then, parting is such sweet sorrow."

Oh no! Had Oscar and Johanna finished their work?

I jumped up, ready to block Capo's path. I'd think of some excuse for keeping him around if I had to. But luckily, I did not. From above, I heard a reassuring coo. Breathing easier, I looked at the big cat and thought to myself, *You're not going anywhere.*

Twenty-Seven

One by one, Capo's feline lieutenants leaped over the hedge to the fence's crossbar, then clambered up and over. Meanwhile, Johanna had returned to the power line to implement Part Four of the plan. With a flutter of her wings, she signaled each time a cat dropped to the alley below: One . . . two . . . three . . . four . . . five . . . .

Five?

Where was six?

Including Capo, there had been seven cats on the patio. By this time, all the others should have left.

Perhaps I had miscounted? Perhaps Dominic was so badly hurt he could not make the leap?

No matter what the explanation was, I had a job to do—Part Five. In anticipation of Capo's next move, I jumped up on the picnic bench and then to the table, where I'd be out of Capo's way. Not that I couldn't take him in a one-on-one fight. That is, I thought I could. The villain had surprised me before.

I assessed the angle of the sun and figured Mutanski would be home soon. At the same time, I heard a terrific yowl, a succession of snarls, hisses and thumps, a screech and finally an exclamation: "Curse you, you unrecalcitrant cur!"

I had never seen Capo move quickly till now when he shot out of the hedge, furious. "What have you done?" he cried when at last he looked up and found me.

"Blocked your exit," I said. Even now, Capo was a formidable enemy, and my voice quavered when I spoke.

All those thumps and bangs must have been the big cat throwing himself against the fence in frustration. Like the Gingham Gang before him, Capo was trapped.

Nose bleeding, eyes puffy, he looked like he had been in a fight, which he had—a fight with a fence.

Now he howled again, calling his gang, trying to bring in reinforcements. It wasn't a command, it was a plea. But there was no reply.

"They've abandoned me, those ingrates!" he howled.

"They can't really help you, you know," I said. "There's no way for them to lift you over the fence. And they can't clear the nest that's plugging up your exit, either. If I know Oscar and Johanna, they have packed the hole as solid as brick."

Unaccustomed to frustration, Capo was suffering. Eyes flashing, he panted and paced, his mind trying to find a means of escape from his predicament.

Meanwhile I was following his every move, still on high alert in case he tried something tricky, when a thin feline voice said, "Ahem."

The sixth cat!

I crossed to the other side of the picnic table, looked down . . . and there in the ivy was the sickly white cat, Pepito.

"Hello," I said politely. "Left behind?"

"Too weak to make it over the fence," he said. "I haven't been well—"

"Oh, thank heavens you're here," said Capo. "Look, first I need you to rip the canine's eyes out, then hop up and see about punching out an exit for me, would you?"

Weak as he was, Pepito kept his voice steady. "I don't think so."

"What did you say? Perhaps I didn't speak loudly enough." Capo started to repeat his orders at higher volume.

Pepito interrupted. "I'm not following orders anymore. The rules have changed. As of now, I am my own cat."

Capo sputtered, stuttered and stomped. "You're a traitor to your species!"

"Look around," said Pepito. "See any cats coming to your rescue? You're on your own, and so am I."

"Uh . . . can I say something?" I tried.

"No!" Capo's manners were not improving.

"Sure," Pepito said to me. "I'd like to know what's going to happen next."

At this moment Capo realized he had nothing to lose. With a scream like an Apache war cry, he jumped from the ground to the bench and then the table.

Eyes hot, tail swishing, claws menacing, he began to advance on my vulnerable nose and flesh.

I stomped my forepaws, dipped my head and leveled out my tail—attack position. In the heroic tradition of my ancestors facing down psychotic badgers, I growled and showed my teeth.

Come and get me, fatso!

At the same time, my allies rallied to the cause. As one, Johanna's flock rose from the telephone wire and circled overhead. Capo was so intent on me he did not notice until one released a gooey mess of recycled bird food that landed with a plop beside his nose.

"*Bleahh!*" Capo's reaction was a reflex. So was his impulse to look up as the winged shadows swooped and whirled around us.

Perhaps he thought of all the chicks and birds his gang had murdered, the eggs and nests they'd smashed. Perhaps at last he was afraid.

The birds diverted Capo just long enough. A moment later, I smelled the distinctive aroma of teenage girl laden with products. Mutanski! Her lips were green that day. Even so, I welcomed her with equal parts joy, relief and gratitude. Just like dashing Colonel Joshua Trueheart himself, she had arrived to save the day.

Twenty-Eight

Now, quick as his girth allowed, Capo dropped to the bench and then the ground before moving in a hurried waddle—belly swinging beneath him—toward the safety of the hedge.

Meanwhile Johanna and her cronies dispersed.

"Rats have mercy!" Mutanski said. "Was that a cat? Where did he come from? And goodness' sake, here's another one. Oh, baby." She shook her head. "You don't look good, and you don't smell so hot either."

Mutanski was right about Pepito. All cats smell putrid, but with his afflictions and more than average filth, Pepito smelled worse than most.

"*Awww*, but I see you're a nice kitty," said Mutanski.

Apparently Pepito had not always been a stray. Now he displayed his people skills, purring, bumping Mutanski's shin, rolling over and batting his paws at the sky.

"But I can't keep you." Mutanski shook her head. "Mom's

allergic—and what happened to your fat, shy friend, anyway? Strudel, do you know anything about this?"

I wagged my tail and played dumb.

I dunno. I dunno. I dunno. I'm only the dog.

There had been glitches, but in spite of them my plan so far had played out successfully. Now it was time for the humans to do their part, Part Six, not that they knew that was what they were doing. Johanna had believed I could predict human behavior. We were about to find out if she was right.

"Well, it doesn't matter," Mutanski continued. "Mom's allergies are so bad that you guys have to go bye-bye and fast. Come on in, Strudel. I'll get you some water and a treat. Do you want a treat? You're a good dog—yes, you are!"

I am, I am, I am! How true!

While I chowed down on a much-deserved biscuit, Mutanski left a phone message for her mom. Then she filled two plastic cereal bowls with water and took them outside. "Do those cats eat dog food, do you think?" she asked me.

Oh yeah, they do.

"Or . . . I know," Mutanski went on. "Maybe Mrs. Rodino has some leftover cat food from Mitzi. Even if it's stale, it's better than nothing. I'll go ask while I'm waiting for Mom to call. You stay here, bud. I'll be right back."

Jake came home a few minutes later, but he didn't find out about the cats till Mutanski returned from Mrs. Rodino's with a plastic yogurt container full of fishy and disgusting cat food.

"Wait, what? Cats? *Where?*" Jake said.

"On the patio, idiot. I just told you!" said Mutanski.

Jake ran to the glass door and grabbed the latch.

"Don't let 'em in! Mom'll kill us!" Mutanski warned.

"I only see one." Jake peered out. "And he's all beat up. Poor guy. I guess it's tough being a stray."

I dipped my nose and stomped my paws.

If either of you wastes any more sympathy on cats, I swear I will leave a mess on the rug!

"What're we gonna do?" Jake continued.

"Mom texted we should call animal control."

"You mean like the dog catcher?"

"Cat catcher," Mutanski said, "but yeah."

"We can't do that! They might . . . *you* know." Jake drew a forefinger across his neck.

I pranced around Jake's ankles.

Go ahead! Call the cat catcher! Call!

"What about Mrs. Rodino?" Jake said.

"I thought of that," said Mutanski.

"You did not!" Jake said. "You just want to take credit for my idea."

"It doesn't take a genius, genius," said Mutanski. "Her cat died, and she likes cats."

"These cats probably aren't even nice," said Jake. "Mom says strays are wild."

"How do you know they're strays?"

"One is—the disgusting one. Nobody would have a cat as ugly as that," Jake said.

"He has a nice personality, though," said Mutanski.

"Something you would know nothing about," said Jake.

"Ha ha. Very funny. So who's gonna go ask Mrs. Rodino? I got the food. It's your turn."

"Come with me?" Jake said. "Please?"

"Oh, all right," Mutanski said. "But let's go before Mom gets home—or Arnie—and calls animal control without ever giving us a chance."

While Jake and Mutanski were gone, I looked out the door at Pepito, who—*gross!*—had claimed my pillow. He looked surprisingly at peace for a cat who might be caught and trucked to a shelter at any moment. Maybe life with the Pier 67 Gang had been so awful that anything else would be an improvement.

Meanwhile, Capo stayed out of sight.

Twenty-Nine

Jake and Mutanski were gone so long that I caught a few well-deserved winks. When they came back, Jake picked me up so I could lick his face. For lunch he had eaten carrots, a turkey sandwich and chocolate milk.

"She says she'll take 'em, Stru!" he told me. "She says she's not afraid of any old stray cat, and I think if anyone can tame 'em, she can. She's always had cats."

"We told her we'd bring 'em over," Mutanski said, "while she gets everything set up. To catch 'em, she says to use pillowcases and gardening gloves."

"And goggles! And hazmat suits! And scuba gear!" said Jake.

Mutanski rolled her eyes and pointed upstairs. "Just get the pillowcases."

The light was fading when, a few minutes later, the kids were ready. Mutanski told me to stay, but Jake contradicted her. "Without Strudel, how will we find the second cat—the shy one?"

Mutanski reconsidered. "Yeah, maybe you're right."

Outside, Pepito barely had time to blink before a pillow-case dropped on him. "Gooood kitty. Niiice kitty." Mutanski tied the pillowcase closed, then picked it up with the squirming cat inside. "Now what do I do with him?"

"Stick him back in the house," Jake said. "He can't get away when he's tied up like that."

As soon as Mutanski came back, I did my best imitation of a pointer to indicate Capo's location in the dark corner by the rosebushes.

"Wouldja look at Strudel!" Jake said.

"He sees something, all right," said Mutanski. "You go over there and check it out. The cat we want is as fat as a bowling ball—one of those gray-and-brown-striped tabbies."

"Oh good. Now I won't grab the wrong cat by mistake." Jake felt around under the rosebushes. It was too dark for him to see, but any second, he was going to get a handful of Capo. Sure enough: *Mrrrow!*

"Bingo!" Jake grabbed as much fur as he could and yanked. The big cat flew toward him, Jake went over backward and a second later he and Capo were wrestling on the ground.

Yow!

Ow!

Owieee!

"Jake, are you okay?" Mutanski danced around, wrung her hands and looked worried.

"Drop the pillowcase on him, wouldja?" Jake spit out the words between grunts. Mutanski dropped the pillowcase, which instantly came to life and escaped Jake's clutches. Now it was tripping, stumbling and somersaulting around the patio like a small, demented ghost.

"Stop him—he'll hurt himself!" Mutanski said.

"Geronimo!" Jake threw himself tummy-down onto the traveling pillowcase. For a moment everything was quiet, then there was a pathetic *mew*, then Jake asked, "Now what do we do?"

"Is he okay?" Mutanski asked.

"He's squirming like he is." Still on the ground, Jake pulled in his arms so that they encircled the bagged cat. Then he brought himself up onto his hands and knees, leaned back and sat up. In his lap, the pillowcase was still.

I would have loved to trash-talk the cruel ex-gang leader as he was being hauled through the house. But I didn't. I remembered how the Gingham Gang had escaped from prison and come back to get revenge on Sheriff Silver. What if Capo got away and the Pier 67 Gang came back for me?

For now, at least, peace and justice had triumphed. Still, it was safer to be gracious in victory.

Thirty

I wanted to celebrate my success.

But there was no one to celebrate with.

My humans had no idea what I had done. Johanna and Oscar were outside while I stayed in. The weather was wintry cold. Walks were short and didn't include the dog park; the news I got was limited.

From my humans, I figured Pepito and Capo were still at Mrs. Rodino's, but how were they getting along there? No one told me.

As for the Pier 67 Gang, their putrid smell lingered on, but without Capo, were they as powerful as they had been before? I asked Rudy when I met him on walks, but he couldn't answer the question.

Twice it snowed hard enough that the snow stayed on the ground, totally transforming the smellscape. Some odors intensified. Any dog can find a stale piece of pizza at the bottom of a snowdrift. But other odors weakened.

Canine messages, for example, are hopelessly garbled when they're frozen.

One Saturday Jake and his grandpa went out in the morning and came back with a Christmas tree. My previous human had had a Christmas tree, too, but his was kept in a box in the closet and smelled like warm plastic and dust. Jake's family's smelled like green things and the outside, only without so much car exhaust and grease.

The tree was put up in the living room. Mutanski took one look, declared she was "too old for this stuff" and left. Mom sighed, then asked Jake if Lisa might want to come over and help decorate.

"There will be cocoa," Mom said, "with marshmallows."

I wagged my tail and looked as adorable as possible.

Cocoa? What's cocoa? Do dogs like cocoa? I'm pretty sure they do! And marshmallows? Dogs love *those. Don't they? Yummy, yummy, yummy!*

When Lisa arrived, Rudy's smell came with her. I wished that he had been invited over for cocoa, too.

The boxes Mom brought up from the dark and scary basement smelled like mildew and spiders. Inside were lights and shiny things for the tree. I had had experience with these things in my previous home, and knew you got in trouble if you ate them. Anyway, they didn't taste that good.

The humans decorated the tree and talked, their boring conversation background noise for my nap on the plaid chair. They were almost done when Lisa said something about the cats that live by the river, and I jerked my head up to listen.

"Traps? What are you talking about?" Jake asked Lisa.

"I heard about the traps, too," Mom said. "Animal

control officers caught dozens of strays. I used to see those cats all the time when I went to the shopping center down there. Poor things. Some of them were pretty, but a lot were scruffy, too."

"But why did they need to trap them?" Jake asked. "Why can't the cats just go on living by the river?"

Now I sat up in my chair and barked.

Because they're cats!

Lisa laughed. "It's almost like Strudel knows we're talking about cats."

I barked again, which made everybody laugh.

Then Mom explained, "It's tough on wildlife when the cat population gets big. They eat baby birds and amphibians and rodents. Also a big feral population, a wild population, carries diseases that can infect house cats."

I woofed again, but quietly. I really loved Mom at that moment, and I loved her even more a few minutes later when she brought out mugs of cocoa for Jake and Lisa, as well as a whole bag of marshmallows.

Cocoa turns out to be chocolate—*bleah!* But it was sugary, too, and the smell was nice. Marshmallows, on the other hand, aren't chocolate at all. Patient and adorable, I sat on the floor beside Jake and gazed up longingly.

All I want's one marshmallow. Just one. Please, please, please?

Sure enough, it worked! Jake slipped me a marshmallow from the bag while Mom was in the kitchen. That marshmallow was heaven itself. Pure sweetness! Tragically, it was gone in an instant. Hey, it's not my fault I eat fast.

I whimpered.

How about one more? Please, please, please?

My human is a good human, but sometimes he can be heartless. "Cut it out, Strudel," he said. "You'll get sick if you eat too many. Oh wow, I just thought of something. If Mutanski and I hadn't taken those two cats over to Mrs. Rodino, maybe they would've been trapped, too."

Thinking of marshmallows, I didn't grasp the meaning of Jake's comment at first. Then I did, and it was enough to make me forget marshmallows . . . almost.

If Jake was right, it meant that my plan hadn't vanquished Pepito and Capo at all. Instead, it had saved them!

What would Oscar and Johanna say when they found that out?

Mom came back from the kitchen, and Lisa asked her what would happen to the cats animal control had trapped.

"The healthier ones, the ones that are friendly, maybe they'll get adopted," Mom said. "The others . . ." She shrugged and shook her head. "Shelters can't afford to keep unwanted animals for long."

Lisa frowned. "That's sad," she said.

I didn't think so . . . until the cats' fate made me think of another unwanted animal: Maisie. Had she been adopted? She was no soulless wicked cat. She was one of the best dogs I ever knew. But maybe the way humans saw it, she was just another unwanted animal.

That night before bed, Jake told me the family was going away on Christmas Day.

"To Uncle Mike's house," he explained. "He's my mom's brother. He lives in the suburbs. Some years he and my mom aren't getting along, but this year I guess they are. Grandpa's coming, too."

Scrunched under the covers, I wiggled my tail.

What about me? Remember me? Am I going to the suburbs? What's a suburbs?

For once, Jake seemed to understand my question. "You

can't come, Strudel. Sorry. Uncle Mike has kind of a fancy house, Mom says, and he is not a dog person. But we'll only be gone for the day. Lisa's coming over to walk you. You like Lisa."

I did like Lisa—so much that on Christmas Day when I heard her outside I didn't bark at all. I waited patiently at the door for it to open, and then I exploded in happy, tail-wagging yips.

Glad to see you! Glad to see you! Merry Christmas! Got any treats?

I ran in circles around her ankles, jumped up against her knees and ran in circles some more. She was carrying a paper bag with something delicious-smelling inside.

Can you believe my family left me here? I am so, so glad to see you! Merry Christmas! What's in the bag? A treat, I bet. Is it a treat?

Lisa scooped me up in her arms, carried me into the kitchen and set the bag down on the counter. "Settle down, Strudel! You must be dying to go out by now. You're a good dog, yes you are! Merry Christmas!"

There was only a little snow left on the ground, and it was freezing cold. There were very few messages at the power pole. Had all the other dogs gone to the suburbs?

Usually I really, really, really love my walk, but that day my paws were turning to ice cubes. I stopped at a convenient tree, then turned around and tugged the leash toward home. I thought Lisa would be ready to turn back, too, but she pulled in the opposite direction.

"Hang on, Stru. I just want to take a couple of puffs. Then we can go back. And guess what—Rudy sent a treat for you for Christmas."

Yes, yes, yes! Oh boy! Oh boy—a treat!

But what did she mean, "a couple of puffs"? I didn't

understand . . . until I smelled something stinky, something that reminded me of Arnie. *Bleah!*

Lisa coughed, and I looked over my shoulder. She had a cigarette in her mouth. She inhaled deeply, coughed again and made a face.

There were always cigarette butts on the sidewalk, but up till then I'd only seen Arnie and a few other grown-up humans smoking. Seeing Lisa do it seemed all wrong. Once again I made the turn toward home and tugged, this time with all my tenacious hound-dog might.

I looked back hopefully and Lisa dropped the cigarette on the sidewalk, stamped it out and grinned. "Okay, Strudel, I'm cold, too. And don't give me that look either. It's not like I'm hooked. It's just a fun thing to do, you know? Something grown-up and cool."

In the bag on the kitchen counter were two treats from Rudy. One was a dog biscuit shaped like the shiny things on the Christmas tree. The biscuit had writing on it, too, but I can't read, and besides it was gone before I got a good look.

The other treat was a red-and-green squeaky toy shaped like a roly-poly Santa. Lisa tossed it for me, then tossed it again. To make her laugh, I chased my tail, then did the sofa-coffee-table-plaid-chair circuit so many times I got dizzy.

Thirty-One

Jake, Mom and Mutanski got home late that night.

"Come on, Strudel," Mom said. "I'll take you out. Jake, you go on up to bed. Call it one last Christmas present."

Jake's nod turned into a yawn. "Thanks, Mom."

When I crawled under the covers a few minutes later, Jake rolled over and hugged me. "It was a really good Christmas," he muttered. There was pie on his breath. Maybe they had brought home leftovers?

"At the last minute, Arnie couldn't make it," Jake went on. "I wish *you* coulda . . ." He yawned again, and his voice trailed off. Soon he was asleep.

Mom had to work the next day; both Jake and Mutanski slept late. Maybe this was nice for them, but it was torture for me. The morning seemed to stretch to infinity. I was hungry and I needed to go out in the worst way.

I tried tugging Jake's covers. I tried licking his face. I tried whining.

If you don't want a cleanup job first thing, you had better get out of bed right now!

"Quit it, Strudel," Jake said. "I'll get up in a sec." Then he rolled over.

With no choice, I barked in his ear, and he opened his eyes like he'd heard an alarm go off. When I barked again, he started to scold me . . . then he looked at the clock.

"Oh gosh! Sorry, Strudel. Come on and I'll take you out for a sec."

Finally, finally, finally!

Jake didn't comb his hair or brush his teeth or even put on clothes. Instead he ran downstairs, tugged on outdoor boots and a coat and clipped the leash to my collar. A moment later we were standing on the sidewalk in the bright, cold sunshine, and I was feeling a lot better.

Then I heard giggling.

It was Lisa, which I knew not only from her voice but from the smell—cigarettes, same as Arnie.

"Hey, Jake," she said. "Did you just get out of bed?"

Jake's embarrassment was so powerful I felt like blushing, too. "Yeah," he said. "I didn't think I'd see anybody. I was only gonna be out here for a sec."

"That's okay. I won't tell," Lisa said. "Rudy and I were out here early, but he wanted to go right back in. He wouldn't even walk around the block. I don't get it. He was wearing the cutest reindeer sweater I gave him for Christmas. He should've been plenty warm."

Jake said, "Maybe his sweater's embarrassing."

"No way!" Lisa said. "It's a *darling* sweater, and anyway dogs don't get embarrassed."

Beg to differ on that point!

All the same, I might have put up with a plain sweater

myself, one without reindeer. It was cold outside for sure, and I wanted to get going. I tugged my leash.

"Yeah, okay, Strudel," Jake said. "We can go around the block. Who cares what I look like?"

"Can I come?" Lisa asked.

"I guess so. I didn't even brush my teeth," Jake said.

"Have you ever heard of *Too Much Information*?" Lisa asked.

We headed away from our house on our usual route. In the sunshine, the smells were powerful and pleasant.

Yum! Doughnut!

I lunged, but Jake was quick and pulled me away.

"It's not good for you, Strudel. Who knows where it's been?"

I do! I know! And doughnuts are good for dogs—trust me!

But Jake was listening to Lisa, not me.

"So, I've got something if you want to try it," she told him.

"Got something what?" he asked. I couldn't see but I knew it was a cigarette like yesterday. She must have pulled it out of her pocket to show him.

"Oh . . . no. Uh, that's okay," said Jake.

"I just mean *try*, it's not like you'll get addicted," she said. "Are you chicken?"

"No!" Jake said. "Of course not. But . . . okay, the thing is, *Arnie* smokes. My mom's boyfriend? And Arnie's not exactly an ad for cigarettes. He's gross."

Jake had paused when he and Lisa started talking, and soon he stopped paying attention to me at all—*Yay! Freedom!*

A dog from out of the neighborhood had left a deposit in the dirt on the edge of the playground, and for once I got the chance to thoroughly investigate . . . until Jake tugged the leash hard. "Strudel! *Ick!* Get away—*gross!*"

Oh, all right. What is that up ahead? A lunch bag? I hope there's more than black banana peels inside.

"Where'd you even get cigarettes, anyway?" Jake asked Lisa. "Your parents don't smoke."

"I got 'em from your pal Anthony," Lisa said. "He gave me a couple to try and then he sold me a couple more."

"Anthony's not my pal," Jake said.

"Sure he is. He says he is," Lisa said. "Anyway, I thought you knew he sold cigarettes. He and that big kid, Richie. It's, like, their business. A lot of kids buy cigarettes from them."

I had run a little way ahead by this time, and Jake must have stopped because I came to the end of the leash with a lurch. "He's trying to get you hooked!" Jake said.

"Don't be dramatic," said Lisa. "Anyway, haven't you wondered what smoking's like?"

Now they were standing still. I looked around for something interesting to sniff. There was a crumpled napkin saturated with human smell, but it wasn't all that tasty. "So go ahead and tell me, if you want," Jake said. "What's smoking like?"

"First you feel kind of green and suffocating, and you cough a lot. But after a few puffs, that part goes away and you feel nice—happy," Lisa said.

Jake said, "Huh. Green and suffocating? Sounds cool, really cool. Anyway, I'm happy enough. Aren't you?"

"It's worth it!" Lisa insisted. Then she seemed to back down. "That is, maybe it's worth it. Anthony charges a dollar each, too. So it's kind of expensive. Anthony's a little scary, don't you think? I'd be careful around him if I were you. It's him that broke the window at Betty's Quik-Stop. Did you know that?"

I had been sniffing an ancient message from Luca, but

145

now Jake made a choking sound in his throat, and I stopped to listen to what he'd say next. "Wh-where'd ya hear that?" Jake asked.

"Around," Lisa said. "Supposedly it's because Betty wouldn't sell him cigarettes. He was mad at her for that. I've tried beer, too. Have you?"

"Sure," Jake said. "I didn't like it. It's bitter. Why does anybody want to drink something bitter? Wait—does Anthony sell beer, too?"

"I don't think so," Lisa said. "That's weird that you didn't know about the cigarettes."

Jake started walking again. We were heading toward home. "Yeah, weird," Jake said. "You know, I could smell the smoke on you, but I thought you'd just been around somebody gross like Arnie."

"Ick," said Lisa.

"Yeah," said Jake. "Ick."

"So anyway, you want some gum?"

Gum, gum, gum! I love gum—especially scraped off the sidewalk with my teeth.

Jake said, "Yeah, sure, gum's okay. Thanks."

"I chew it to hide the smell. That way my parents don't suspect about the smoking," Lisa said.

"I bet they suspect anyway," Jake said. "I mean, the smoke's on your clothes. Gum doesn't do anything about that."

"Oh," Lisa said. "Really?"

"Yeah, Lisa. Really," said Jake.

To that I added, *Woof.*

Thirty-Two

That night before he fell asleep, Jake rolled over and rubbed my tummy. "So now the whole thing makes sense, huh, Strudel?"

Here's a funny thing about my human. Sometimes he'll start a conversation in the middle like I'm supposed to know what he's been thinking. Usually if I wait he explains, and that's what happened that night, too.

"Anthony and Richie are just big bullies, Strudel," he continued. "They paid me to break Betty's window because they couldn't get cigarettes from her. And Betty's nice, too. So's Lisa. What they're doing makes me mad, Strudel. Does it make you mad, too?"

Sure, sure, sure, Jake! If you're mad—me, too. Only . . . can we go to sleep now?

"It's funny that Lisa'd be smoking, 'cause she's smart," he went on. "Her grades are a ton better than mine, and my mom says her parents have money. They could send her to a fancy rich-kids school, only they think the public one's more normal."

Jake sighed and shifted one more time under the covers.

"Maybe her parents don't know about kids like Anthony," he mumbled. "Or maybe there're kids like him at fancy schools, too."

The next day was Thursday, and Arnie came to dinner. While he and my humans ate in the kitchen, I made myself comfortable in the plaid chair. From there I'd be well positioned to make a raid on the kitchen floor just as soon as they got up from the table. There might be something left. Sometimes a dog gets lucky.

Dinner was spaghetti, one of Jake and Mutanski's favorites.

"It's great, Mom," Jake said.

"Great," said Mutanski with her mouth full.

After that they were too busy slurping noodles to talk.

Mom announced she was going to work early the next day, New Year's Eve. "People need our help sprucing up for their parties," she said.

"But what about *our* New Year's Eve?" Arnie asked. "I was thinking maybe your dad could watch the bambinos while you and I take a quick trip to Atlantic City."

"Arnie," Mom said, "sometimes I honestly wonder what planet you live on. Dad's a Mummer, remember? He's busy from now through New Year's night. It's not just preparations and parade, it's the twenty-four-hour parties on 2 Street, too."

"Oh yeah, I forgot about that," said Arnie. "Traffic will be a mess with the streets blocked off."

Mom sighed. "It's the noise that gets me. Dad swears they're going to keep it down this year, but I'll believe that when I hear it."

The winter weather meant I had to spend every day inside. By Friday I was going slightly crazy, but Jake seemed entirely happy with endless video games and snacks.

Around lunchtime Mutanski told him, "There's snow coming tonight, you know. You oughta take your beast out for a good walk now."

"You're not the boss of me," Jake said from his perch on the sofa. There was a bowl of taco chips beside him. Every time he got up, I snagged a couple. So far he hadn't noticed.

"I'm just saying—" Mutanski began.

"Yeah, well don't say," Jake said. "He's my dog. I'm responsible for him."

"Okaaay," said Mutanski.

And so I waited. And waited.

It was almost dark and the taco chips were gone when Jake stretched, looked out the window, saw the streetlights were on and realized we still hadn't gone for a walk.

"Shoot, Strudel. I'm sorry!" he said.

I was sitting by the door before he even got up from the sofa.

Outside, the cold was the kind that seeps into your bones, and snow had begun to fall. The pavement beneath my paws was icy. Some people had salted their walks, and the salt grains stuck between my toes and burned.

I didn't care. I was so *happy happy happy* to be outside at last!

When a few moments later I spotted Luca, I was happier still. He was with Anthony, but I was so glad to see another dog that I could ignore that part.

I wagged like crazy and charged forward to get a good thorough sniff.

Hello! Hello! Hello!

Meanwhile the big puppy had his tongue lolling out and his head down; he was as desperate to play as I was.

I should've been prepared for Jake to pull me back, but I wasn't and—*owie! My neck!* Then Anthony yanked Luca, too, and as hard as we tried we could not get close enough to nose each another.

So near and yet so far. It was agony!

"Hey, I got a bone to pick with you, punk," Anthony said to Jake. "I told you about that new job, and it's like ever since I did, you've been making yourself scarce. Am I right?"

"No," said Jake. "That is, yes. I don't want to do that job for you. I won't do it. He's my grandpa. It's not right you should ask me."

Sometimes Jake whined when he talked to Anthony, but not this time. Even though I could smell the fear on his skin, his voice was firm.

"So you don't wanna steal from your grandpa, is that it?" Anthony said. "That makes you a good boy, Jakey. But lemme tell ya somethin'. A few dollars out of the cash box is nothin' to a bakery that does so much business. Your grandpa'll never miss it, and Richie and I will put it to good use."

"I found out about the cigarettes," Jake said. "I found out you're even selling to kids my age, like Lisa."

"Yeah? So? Can't Lisa make her own decisions?" Anthony said.

"I don't like it," said Jake.

"You liked the money, didn't you?"

Jake didn't answer.

"You took it, and now you owe us."

"I did what you asked, and you paid me, and now we're done," Jake said. There was a tremor in his voice. I wondered if Anthony could hear it, too.

"What if it was to get out that *you're* the one who threw that rock through Betty's window?" Anthony asked.

"You said I wouldn't get in trouble," Jake reminded him.

"I could've been wrong about that," said Anthony. "Or here's another possibility. What if I was to decide to sic this guy on you? You and your mutt? I don't like to think what Luca'd do to that pipsqueak—especially if he tried to run for it. My dog's got a taste for cowards' blood."

This was nonsense, but still I set my front paws, shifted my weight back and looked the big puppy in the eye. Goaded by his human, Luca might try something. If he did, I wanted to be ready.

Never underestimate the little dog.

"So Jakey," Anthony went on, "now that I've clarified the situation, what do you say? Look, I'll even give you a couple of days to bring me the cash. It's the holidays, after all. I can be generous."

Luca strained at the leash and yipped. Anthony probably thought he was after blood, but I knew he was after playtime.

"I say no," Jake said, and square-jawed or not, he sounded just like Sheriff Silver.

I was very proud . . . for about one second, because that's when Anthony let go of Luca's leash and the big dog lunged.

Thirty-Three

A lifetime being a little dog has taught me something about big ones. Most of them never expect to be challenged. Most of them have low tolerance for pain and bloodshed, at least when the blood is their own.

Well, that's not the way we dachshunds roll. We mix it up and ask for more. There're plenty of things worse than a few tooth marks in your hide, and one is failing to do your job. My job was to protect my human.

When Luca came at me, his heart wasn't in it.

But I charged with everything I had—yanking the leash from Jake's hand, baring my teeth, growling, snapping and generally reminding the big puppy that I was the alpha dog here.

The moment Luca saw the whites of my canines, he leaned left, spun on his paws and took off in the opposite direction . . . with me on his tail, yipping up a storm.

"Don't bite me!" Luca shouted over his shoulder.

"You scared my human," I called back. "What's he ever done to you?"

For two blocks I chased the overgrown puppy in the swirling snow, my leash trailing behind me. I had spent the whole day napping indoors; running felt wonderful.

By this time I had lived in the neighborhood for months. I thought I knew its every sound and smell, but soon I came to a street I didn't recognize. It should've been the one called 2 Street, the one with the store that smells like doughnuts and chicken.

Now the luscious odor of grease remained, but everything else was different. Two Street had been transformed!

I felt panic rising, and the frightening reality shift that Maisie called a "flashback." Colored lights swirled around me, and crowds, and so many cars and trucks that I could hardly make my way.

And the humans! They smelled of alcohol and tobacco smoke. They didn't look normal at all. Some were wearing shiny, bright costumes. Some had painted faces. Everywhere music blared, competing tunes that together made an ugly muddle of noise that hurt my head.

All at once I longed for my own humans. I longed for home. I longed for Jake.

Where was he? Was he safe?

Was I safe?

I dodged the wheels of cars and the legs of humans. Twice someone got hold of my leash to stop me—"Here, doggie, doggie! Come back, doggie, doggie!"—but I yanked free and kept going.

It was lucky that Luca was a tall dog. I kept his tail in sight.

Under a car I scooted, then across a sidewalk and down

a narrow street, away from the light and the noise. Still running, Luca was only a few yards ahead. At last I could breathe again.

"Hey, Luca!" I called. "Could we give it a rest? My legs aren't as long as yours!"

Obediently the big dog slowed to a trot and stopped. When he turned to face me he dipped his snout, acknowledging my alpha-dog status. He was panting. "I thought you'd never stop chasing me."

"What do you mean, you big goofball?" I laid my ears back and body bumped him to say no hard feelings. "I stopped chasing you a long time ago! I was trying to keep up. Where are we, anyway?"

"Search me," said Luca.

"Wait, you're lost, too? But you've lived here longer than me."

"I don't get walked much," Luca said. "My human complains every time we go out."

"Gee, that's tough," I said.

"I'm cold," he said. "Can we go home now?"

"Sure." I gave a good shake to get the snowflakes off my back. "We can re-sniff our steps. Only, what was that over on 2 Street? I don't mind telling you, the noise, the colors—the whole thing made me nervous."

Luca sat back and scratched at a fleabite. Unlike me, he didn't seem bothered. I guess some dogs' senses aren't as sharp as a dachshund's. "Crazy human stuff," he said. "Who cares? Did you notice the treat potential? Let's go see what's to eat, want to?"

Even amidst the confusion of smells, it didn't take us long to sniff our way back to 2 Street.

Luca quivered with puppy excitement. "Pepperoni!" he yelped. "And how about that—nacho cheese! Yummy,

yummy, yummy! Are those biscotti? Don't you love biscotti?"

"I thought you wanted to go home, Luca. I thought you were cold."

"I am, I am, I am—but a dog has to eat! I think maybe I'm still growing."

Just to keep Luca company, I sniffed out half a hoagie from the gutter and took a good-sized bite. I was enjoying the taste of spoiled mayonnaise when I heard the first *crack,* then the second and then a colossal *boom*. The sounds seemed to wash over me like wind—making my bones vibrate and my brain throb.

In an overwhelming wave, the terror of the calamity came back. Panic rose in my chest, and I could not keep it down. It was happening again—apocalypse!

I had to escape. I had to!

Head down, tail down, nose straight ahead, I ran without looking back.

Thirty-Four

From behind me, I heard Luca calling, "Strudel—come this way!"

I kept on running.

The rough ice on the pavement tore my paws, and the salt made them sting. The wet snow froze my nose. Brakes squealed and car horns blared. People shouted, "Dog! What're ya doin'? Get outta the street!" Someone tried to step on my trailing leash, but I was too fast. I don't know for how long I ran. I only stopped because my chest was heaving and my legs burned like fire. I could not take another step.

Only then did I realize that the awful sounds had faded into silence.

Was the apocalypse over? What had happened on 2 Street? Was Luca all right? What about my humans?

Maisie's words came back to me: *Summon your hound-dog nature, Strudel.*

Okay, Maisie, I thought. My ancestors had fought badgers. They never gave up. And I wouldn't give up either.

But where was I? And what should I do next?

A few sniffs told me I had come to a strange neighborhood, one I had never walked in before. It looked like Jake's but lacked the charm of smelly and abundant litter. Brick row houses lined both sides of the street, their front doors three steps up from the sidewalk.

In the midst of my ordeal, new memories from the night of the calamity came back. I had run like this then, too. And I had been on a sidewalk in a neighborhood I didn't know, with smells I didn't know. I remembered the rain and the wind. I remembered that the pads of my paws were soaked and sore and bleeding. I remembered being tired—so tired—as if I'd run for miles.

Then, all of a sudden, I had sensed something familiar, a powerful canine smell. I had stumbled toward it and found a spot that was out of the rain. Grateful, I had collapsed, exhausted.

Abruptly I realized that I was remembering how I had come to the shelter! I had run away from the calamity, and sensed the shelter when I was near it. I had lain down in the doorway, which was out of the rain. Shira had taken me in.

Maybe I could find a doorway now. I needed to rest and to think. How was I going to get home?

A dog lived in the house whose doorway I chose, a Maltese from the smell of her. Climbing the three steps to the stoop was like climbing a mountain, but at the top there was a doormat for me to lie down on. It was bristly but the part nearest the door was dry. It was shielded from the wind by flowerpots. I dozed until . . . oh miracle! Jake's voice woke me.

"Strudel! Here, Strudel! Are you out there, buddy? Where are you?"

Exhaustion forgotten, I jumped up and tripped down the steps so fast my paws barely made contact. On the sidewalk I looked right and left before spotting my human halfway down the block. In a moment, Jake's familiar hands were pulling me to his chest.

I licked his face in relief and gratitude.

"Quit it, Strudel!" Jake said, but I knew he didn't mean that. His voice was hoarse from calling me and husky with happy tears, too. "I can't believe I found you. First you chased Luca away—you should've seen Anthony's face! But why did you run so far?

"Okay, time to go home, only there's one slight problem. Where is home, anyway? I think the river's that way . . . or maybe . . ." He turned around, then turned around again.

The warmth of Jake's body revived me, and when I realized he was lost, my hound-dog determination kicked in. I had a job to do.

I wiggled, and Jake put me down. "Good thing you've still got your leash," he said, "and this time I'm not letting go."

Back on the sidewalk, I raised my nose and sniffed the air. From far away came the sharp scent of burning left by the 2 Street destruction. It was the last place I wanted to go, but it was also the direction from which I had come, the direction of home.

Jake resisted my tugging at first, but then he shrugged and gave in.

"Your guess is as good as mine," he said. "At least the snow has stopped."

Here is something I learned that night: Fear makes everything difficult.

Now that my fear had passed, backtracking turned out to be easy. Approaching my own neighborhood at last, I had never been so glad to smell anything. This was my territory, my home,

Amazingly, when we got back to 2 Street the human confusion called a party was still going on. I had expected the street to look like the scenes in Jake's video game, the buildings and vehicles reduced to smoking ruins, but it didn't at all. Except for people in shiny costumes dancing and carrying on, everything looked just fine.

Something had happened that I did not understand. Maybe someday it would be explained. For now, the overload of sights, smells and sounds on 2 Street acted like a beacon for my canine senses. Jake, being only human, hadn't heard a thing till we were less than a block away.

"We're almost back now, Strudel," Jake said when we turned the corner. "Oh gosh, Mom is gonna kill me."

Thirty-Five

Jake couldn't have been more wrong about Mom. Instead of killing him, she burst into tears and hugged us both like she'd never ever let go. Even Mutanski cried. For once she wasn't wearing any lipstick at all. She looked pretty, like somebody whose name was Laura.

"Call your grandpa, honey," Mom said to her. "He's been worried sick."

"Mom, I love you, too, but you gotta let me go." Jake squirmed to get out of her arms. "Strudel's paws are bloody, see that? I'm gonna clean him up and wrap him in a blanket or something."

Mom said okay, she would make cocoa. "And wrap yourself in a blanket, too," she added.

Jake's doctoring was as gentle as Shira's had been. He rubbed me down good, then sprayed all four paws with bad-smelling stuff—*Owie! Owie! Owie! Owie!* He even wiped my tail. Set free at last, I trotted all around the home

160

place doing a quick inspection for signs of apocalypse. I am happy to report I found none.

I was downstairs with Mom and Mutanski in the kitchen, hoping for falling marshmallows, when I heard human sounds outside the front door. In a heartbeat, I was sounding the alarm.

Danger! Danger! Danger!

"Only me, Strudel, boy," Grandpa said as he opened the door and came in. "I'm glad your voice is working good, at least. Hello?" he called. "Did someone say something about cocoa?"

"In here, Dad," Mom called.

Grandpa stomped the ice off his boots and hung his coat on a hook by the door. Then he picked me up and carried me into the kitchen. He had never picked me up before, so I licked his cheek to let him know it was okay. His skin tasted funny, and when Mom got a look at Grandpa she laughed.

"There's still streaks of paint on your face, Dad," she said.

Grandpa set me down and rubbed his cheek. "I was out with the Frogs till I got your call that Jake was missing," he said. "I changed my clothes and washed in a hurry—too big a hurry, I guess. Then I went out looking for my grandson with a couple of buddies of mine. We must've gone the wrong way, though."

Jake came in wearing his pajamas. Grandpa started to punch his shoulder, then turned the punch into a hug. I didn't like being left out, so I used my last reserves of strength to dash around their ankles and yip. This made everybody laugh.

Soon the family was sitting around the table with their

cocoa. For once Mom let me sit in Jake's lap, and kept quiet when he slipped me a marshmallow.

Yummy, yummy, yummy! One more? How 'bout two?

"Now tell your story," Mom said to Jake. "What happened? Where'd you go?"

Jake took a big gulp of cocoa, then wiped his mouth with the back of his hand. "So, okay, Anthony and I were talking, and his dog—you know him, the pit bull? He went after Strudel."

Mutanski narrowed her eyes. "Why did he do that, exactly?"

"Um . . . I dunno," Jake said.

"Hmm," said Mutanski.

Mom asked, "So then what happened?"

I wagged my tail and sat up a little straighter. This next part was going to be good.

"Strudel attacked right back!" Jake said. "It was like he was all of a sudden a wolverine or something—fierce! It would've been scary if it hadn't been Strudel. And Luca—this part was funny—he just turned tail and took off like a shot. You should've seen Anthony's face. He turned bright red, he was so embarrassed."

Mutanski laughed. "Remember that time when Arnie called Luca 'the enforcer'? So I guess he got *that* wrong."

"Can we leave Arnie out of this?" Mom said.

"Where is your paramour this New Year's Eve?" Grandpa asked.

"What's a paramour?" Jake said before Mom could answer.

"Her *boy*friend," said Mutanski.

Mom shook her head and frowned. "Leave him out of this, I said. He's in Atlantic City."

"That so?" said Grandpa.

"All right, Dad. Don't give me that look," said Mom.

"What am I supposed to do? Close my eyes?" said Grandpa.

"Never mind," said Mom. "We still haven't heard the rest of the story. Then what happened, Jake?"

"Well, I chased 'em and almost caught up over on 2 Street, the big New Year's Eve party, but then a bunch of firecrackers popped, and you should've seen Strudel take off. I didn't know he could move so fast."

Mom looked down at me. "Very sensible, Strudel. I don't like loud noises either."

"I had a dog like that when I was a kid," said Grandpa. "He hated anything that went *boom*—thunderstorms, too. He used to hide in a closet."

"What happened to Luca?" Mom asked.

"He was too busy chowing down on something to care about the noise," Jake said, "and Anthony was right behind me anyway. I took off after Strudel, only there were so many people I couldn't see him anymore."

"It was a mob scene over there," Grandpa agreed.

"I kept calling and running," said Jake, "till I didn't know where I was anymore. And I was freezing cold."

"What happened to your phone?" Mom asked.

Jake seemed reluctant to answer this question. When he finally spoke, he looked at me instead of his mom. "Dropped it?"

Mom closed her eyes and shook her head. It was the middle of the night. She was tired and pale. "Jacob Dominic Allegro," she said. "I just don't know about you sometimes. Your phone is gone?"

"It wasn't my fault!" Jake insisted. "It was Strudel's. He yanked it out of my hand."

Luckily for me, Mom was not buying this argument.

"And didn't anyone ever tell you the streets are numbered? How could you possibly get yourself lost?"

"Give him a break, Mom," said Mutanski. "It was dark, and not *all* the streets are numbered. He lost track of the river. He got turned around. I think he went clear up to Society Hill—that's, like, three neighborhoods away."

Mom sighed. "All right. Sheesh, what a time for my kids to gang up on me. So anyway, how did you get back?"

"I found Strudel, or he found me—I'm not sure which," Jake said. "And I guess his sense of direction's better. He was still trailing his leash, and as soon as I picked it up, he led me straight back home."

Thirty-Six

Just like Chief, I had prevailed over evil; peace and justice had been restored.

There was only one problem: Anthony. When Luca ran away from me—the *little* dog, the *runt*, the *pipsqueak*—Anthony was embarrassed. And now Jake was afraid that his embarrassment would turn into anger and a desire for revenge.

Every time we went for a walk, Jake said, "We got to avoid Anthony no matter what, Strudel. You keep a lookout, and so will I."

What he should've said was keep a sniffout, but anyway I got the point.

A week passed. Jake and Mutanski went back to school.

On a sunny Saturday morning, Jake took me out and I found a greeting at power pole central. It was from Luca, and it was only a few minutes old.

Uh oh. I looked back at Jake and yipped.

Wanna go home? Let's go home. How 'bout we go home right now?

As usual, Jake didn't understand. Then, before I could say more, here came Anthony and Luca, and they were heading up the sidewalk straight for us.

When I barked—*Danger, danger, danger*—Jake got the message.

"Shoot," he murmured. He was holding his breath.

But then something surprising happened.

Anthony and Luca crossed the street. They were trying to avoid us!

When Jake told this story to Mutanski later that morning, she nodded. "Of course. What did you expect?"

"I expected to be smeared on the sidewalk like a bug!" said Jake. "What do you mean 'of course'?"

"Little bro, let me explain," said Mutanski. "Luca was supposed to be Anthony's muscle, right? Only he isn't. He's a sweet, mild-mannered baby, and now the whole neighborhood knows it, too."

"They do?" Jake said. "But I only told Lisa and a couple of the other guys. . . ."

"And I only told Ty and Jennica and Briana," said Mutanski. "And each one of them told somebody who told somebody else. Get it?"

"I guess," said Jake, but he still sounded confused.

"Look," said Mutanski, "Anthony and his pal Richie were trying to be like some big powerful force around here with all their business enterprises. But part of that depended on people being scared of Luca. Now because of Strudel, nobody's scared of Luca, and Anthony and Richie look like the idiots they are."

"I don't know how long it'll last," Mutanski continued, "but for now, anyway, the two of 'em are lying low."

166

Jake still seemed worried. "Laura, are you sure?" he asked.

"Yes, Jacob." She grinned. "I am sure."

That night Jake started a conversation in the middle again. I had to think fast to keep up. "Now you and me could strut around the neighborhood, Strudel," he said. "With Anthony and Luca out of the way, we could dominate. What do you think? Are you up for it?"

Woof, I said, meaning *Nope, not really, but you're the boss.*

"How about if we read a little?" Jake asked. "I'm not that tired yet, and tomorrow's Sunday."

Chief, Dog of the Old West

Rachel Mae tore open the crate from Sears and Roebuck only to be bitterly disappointed. The spyglass was on back order. The hot-air balloon was puny, suitable not for flying but for decorating the mantelpiece. As for the net, it might catch a butterfly but never a villain.

"Phooey!" exclaimed Rachel Mae, then she stomped off to her bedroom and slammed the door. Lately it seemed that none of her plans went right.

Now began a period of dark days around the old home place.

Not only was Sheriff Silver's brainy, blue-eyed daughter in a funk, a new menace had reared its ugly, bewhiskered and big-eared head. This menace was a mouse that had laid waste to the grain stores in the pantry.

"Do something, Sheriff!" Chef Pierre cried in frustration. "The rodent will soon be better fed than we are."

"He may have eluded your traps, Chef Pierre," said square-jawed Sheriff Silver, "but he will be no match for our loyal, sleek and powerfully built canine. Get 'im, Chief!"

But Chief did not get 'im. Instead, he whimpered and ran to hide under Rachel Mae's pink-quilted bed.

"Sacre bleu!" exclaimed Chef Pierre. "The brave canine hero is afraid of a tiny mouse!"

The mouse's ongoing campaign of pillage caused nerves to fray like chewed burlap on bags of grain. Meanwhile, the dark cloud of despondency continued to rain down on Rachel Mae.

Then one day Sheriff Silver had an idea.

"Daughter," he said over luncheon, "your family needs you to devise a plan to dispose of the menace that has shattered the peace of our happy home. Only you can do it, Rachel Mae. Will you? Will you help us?"

"Say please," said Rachel Mae.

"Please," said the sheriff.

"S'il vous plaît," said Chef Pierre, reverting to his native language.

As the sheriff had expected, this was just the problem to engage the brain of the brainy, blue-eyed girl. The dark cloud lifted. The sun shone in. Rachel Mae smiled.

"All right, Pa," she said. "I will."

After a day and a sheaf of graph paper, Rachel Mae announced that her plan was complete.

"Does it require telegraph lines?" her pa asked her. "And steamships and the 11th Cavalry and dashing Colonel Joshua Trueheart?"

"It does, Pa," said Rachel Mae. "And the spyglass on back order from Sears and Roebuck, too."

"Well, darlin', that's wonderful," said Pa. "Now tell me all about it. And don't leave out a single thing."

With Rachel Mae busy describing the details, Chef Pierre chased down the mouse, trapped him in the butterfly net and deposited him outside among his prairie-dog cousins.

The chef had just returned to his pots and pans when the household's tranquility was once again disturbed by an intruder bursting in through the front door.

"Stagecoach robbers!" cried the intruder, who was none other than Nellie Bly Bumsted herself.

From Rachel Mae's room down the hall came the sound of a sleek and powerfully built canine scrambling out from under the bed.

"Are you ready, Chief?" Sheriff Silver asked.

Woof, said Chief. And the two of them strode purposefully out onto the prairie, ready to restore peace and justice once again.

Jake closed the book and sighed. "That was a surprising one, wasn't it, Strudel? Who expected a sleek and powerfully built dog like Chief to be afraid of mice? But maybe everyone's afraid of something, Strudel—even canine heroes."

Thirty-Seven

Things were pretty tranquil around my own old home place that winter. Jake and Mutanski went to school. Mom went to work. Arnie came to dinner most nights, and Grandpa brought pizza on Fridays.

There were no breaks from the cold weather, so I didn't go outside during the day. I missed Oscar and Johanna; I looked forward to seeing them again when the weather warmed up.

One Thursday after school, Mom came home early from work. She was making a special dinner, she told Jake. Arnie was bringing company.

"It's all kind of mysterious, Stru," Jake told me. "It's some guy he just met, and he wants the guy to meet us, too, but he won't say why. He says he especially wants the guy to meet *you.*"

Jake smelled anxious, but I was not. Perhaps this fellow had heard how I had prevailed over both feline and human bullies. Perhaps he was an author like Thesiger Sheed Lewis, and he wanted to write my life story.

Thinking about this, I became more and more excited as the afternoon wore on. I ran in circles and chased my tail. I did the sofa-coffee-table-plaid-chair circuit at least three times.

Mutanski said I was in every way a total nuisance. Then she scratched me behind the ears—*awww*.

As usual, I heard human footsteps at the front door long before anyone else did, and I made an announcement.

Company! Hey, hey, hey—company! Alert, alert, alert!

"Enough, Strudel!" Mom said, which was her way of telling me what a good dog I am. Then Jake grabbed me under my belly and pulled me into his arms, which was his way of saying the same thing.

I licked his face.

"*Ewww!* Enough, Strudel!"

I know, Jake, I love you, too.

The door opened and a gust of Arnie's unpleasant scent blew in, followed by Arnie himself. He was laughing and talking to the man behind him.

When that second human scent reached my nostrils, I felt my heart miss a beat.

It couldn't be. It wasn't possible.

But it was!

I squirmed so hard to get down that Jake had to drop me. I was hysterical with joy—jumping, nipping, barking, running in all directions, running around the cuffs of his trousers the same way I did when I was a puppy.

Arnie started to laugh. "I guess he remembers you, all right. That about clinches it as far as ID goes."

As Jake was saying, "Wha . . . ? Who? I don't get it," I was being lifted into my previous human's arms.

He wasn't dead! He was right here!

I licked his face, and he pushed me away gently, just the way he always did. He had never liked having his face licked. But he was laughing and giving me good friendly squeezes and tickles behind my ears. He was glad to see me, too.

There was just one thing. My previous human (who turned out not to be dead) smelled like all the old familiar things—leather, aftershave lotion, dusty carpets and books. But he also smelled like something else: *dog.*

And I had the feeling I knew this dog, too. Her scent was like sugary tea, but I couldn't place her. She was a dog I hadn't smelled in a very long time.

A few minutes later, when the humans sat down to eat dinner, I realized Jake and Mutanski weren't happy about my previous human's return. At first I didn't understand why not.

Then it came to me: They were afraid he would take me away!

And would he?

All of a sudden my joy turned upside down. If my previous human tried to take me from Jake, I wouldn't go. I would plant my paws firmly on the plaid chair. I would hide under the bed. I would do whatever it took to stay with my family.

Even with Arnie at the table, I stayed under Jake's chair during dinner. I wanted to hear every word of the conversation.

"Tell Professor Wagstaff how you happened to get to know Strudel," Mom said to Jake once the plates were served and everyone was sitting down.

Jake explained how his teacher had assigned him to read to animals at the shelter, how he had read me *Chief,*

Dog of the Old West because those stories were his grand-pa's favorites.

"Why, I read those books myself," said Professor Wag-staff. "When I was your age, I thought all the wisdom you'd ever need in life could be found in them."

"I don't know about wisdom," Jake said. "I just like 'em 'cause they're exciting. Lots of action."

For a few minutes the human talk was boring, in other words about subjects that weren't either treats or me. Then Mutanski said, "I still don't get it, Arnie. How did you find Professor Wagstaff, anyway?"

"I didn't go looking for him, if that's what you're think-ing," Arnie said.

"Sheer chance," said Professor Wagstaff. "We share the same barber in Queen Village."

"That's right," said Arnie. "And when I mentioned my girlfriend's kid had a dachsie that ran away from the fire-crackers on New Year's Eve, my barber said he had another client with a dachsie that ran away in a thunderstorm, jumped out the window, lost his collar in the process. But that dachsie never came back."

Professor Wagstaff picked up the story. "The barber mentioned all this to me, too, and I thought about the tim-ing. It seemed just possible that the two dogs were one and the same. So I asked him to give Arnie my phone number, and Arnie invited me along tonight. It wasn't until I saw Mitty, though—or more accurately, till Mitty saw me—that I was sure."

Mitty used to be my name, but I had vowed not to think of it again. I didn't like it any more than I liked Strudel. Nei-ther one of them is heroic enough to suit a badger-fighter.

Now Jake repeated it. "Mitty?"

Professor Wagstaff laughed. "He was named after a

fictional character named Walter Mitty, a man who day-dreamed a lot. Even as a puppy, Mitty aspired to do great things."

I thumped my tail.

That part's right. I did.

"Seems funny he'd be scared to death of a little old thunderstorm, then," said Arnie. There was a smirk in his voice.

"Not at all," said Professor Wagstaff. "Every hero has his tragic weakness, his Achilles' heel, if you will. That's the nature of heroes. Loud noises seem to be Mitty's."

Wait . . . loud noises? Thunder? Hadn't Grandpa mentioned firecrackers on 2 Street as well?

So the calamity had been only a thunderstorm. That was the apocalypse I had escaped.

No wonder there had been no rubble and ruin in our neighborhood. No wonder Professor Wagstaff had survived.

Boy, did I feel foolish.

But then Chief was afraid of a mouse, wasn't he? Maybe Professor Wagstaff was right. Maybe to be a hero, you have to have a weakness.

Jake had been talking, and now I realized he was telling the story of how I prevailed over Luca and led Jake himself back home.

Listening to all this praise, I tried to remain humble, but my tail did not. It was wagging itself.

Then Mom's fork dropped *clink* onto her plate. "Jake, are you saying Arnie's nephew, Anthony, *threatened* you with his pit bull? You never told me that part."

Under his chair, Arnie scuffed his shoes like he was uncomfortable about something.

At the same time, Jake realized he had said too much.

"Aw, it was no big deal, Mom. Just, you know, neighbor-hood stuff. But still. Strudel was real brave."

"We will talk more about this later," Mom said, and it seemed to me she sounded a lot like square-jawed Sheriff Silver.

"You call him Strudel?" Professor Wagstaff said.

"They named him at the shelter," Jake said. "I was going to rename him, but by now Strudel's kind of stuck."

"Oh yes, that's another coincidence—that you found him at the shelter in Old City," Professor Wagstaff said. "After Mitty disappeared, I adopted a dog from the same one. It's odd to think that if I had gone there sooner, I would have found him myself. But I wasn't ready for a new dog right away. I was too broken up.

"When Mitty disappeared, I looked everywhere," he continued. "I called the police and my neighbors. I hung Lost Dog signs on the power poles. But it never occurred to me that Mitty would run as far as he did. He was my pam-pered pet. I had no idea he was that strong.

"Finally, in October, I realized I was lonely, and I thought I could take on a new dog. That's when, at last, I adopted my dear little Maisie."

Maisie! That was the sugary tea smell on Professor Wagstaff!

I inhaled deeply to confirm it. Aw, Maisie. She had found the perfect home for her quiet tastes and temperament.

But I didn't want to join her—not now. I was still a young dog.

Besides, this was where I was needed. For now, peace and justice had won out around here. But like Chief, I had to remain vigilant. Anthony might threaten Jake again. The Pier 67 Gang might find a new boss.

And who could tell what new menaces might lurk just over the horizon?

With a terrible scraping squeak, Mom pushed her chair back from the table and stood up. "Wait one minute," she said. "Is that what this is all about, Arnie? Have you brought Professor Wagstaff here to take Strudel away from us? I know you never liked him, but this . . ."

Arnie was flustered. "Well, Strudel—that is, *Mitty*—is the professor's dog. He paid good money for a purebred puppy, had him brought from a breeder halfway around the world"—

Was this true? I couldn't remember my puppyhood clearly. But it did make sense. Obviously I was a very valuable canine

—"and it's only fair his rightful owner should reclaim him."

Like a dog readying to attack, Mom set her feet squarely beneath her. "If ever there was a more clueless ninny than you, Arnie, I can't imagine who it would be! No offense to Professor Wagstaff, but Strudel is our dog now, and we love him. It would break my heart to take him away from Jake—"

"And from me!" said Mutanski.

"*And* from Laura," said Mom. "If it's a question of money—"

"Uh, may I speak?" Professor Wagstaff broke in.

Mom took a breath. "Please do."

"If Arnie's expectation was that I should reclaim Strudel, I assure you that it wasn't mine," the professor said. "He's a fine, fine animal, and we were the best of friends, weren't we, Mitty?" My former human peeked under the table at me. I smiled and woofed my assent.

Professor Wagstaff smiled back. "But he's also a bit— how should I put it? Energetic? I think a young family

176

such as yours is a better fit. Maisie and I are getting along famously."

"Oh." Arnie sounded disappointed.

"Thank you!" said Jake. "But I bet Strudel would like to have a playdate sometime. Wouldn't you, Stru?"

Woof, I said again. I was thinking how much I'd like to see Maisie. And I was thinking of butter cookies.

Thirty-Eight

Later that night, long after Jake and I had gone to bed, the sounds of snapping and snarling awakened me, human snapping and snarling—Mom and Arnie. Jake didn't wake up, but the fight sounded bad to me.

Since then, Arnie hasn't come over to dinner once, but Grandpa eats with us more often. Sometimes he brings Betty Rossi, the lady who owns Betty's Quik-Stop. When she brings me a treat, it's the premium kind. She is a nice human. Jake says one of these days he's going to muster up his courage and confess that he's the one who threw the brick.

On a Saturday in late March, Jake arranged to meet Professor Wagstaff and Maisie at the dog park. The weather had warmed up during the previous few days. The ground was no longer frozen, and a few brave green shoots were emerging from the gray-brown mud.

At the park, the professor and Maisie were waiting by

the gate. Lisa and Rudy happened to be there, too, and Jake introduced everybody.

"What is it you call this again?" Professor Wagstaff asked. "A doggie play date?"

Lisa laughed. "That's exactly right. Rudy and Strudel are great friends. And even though Strudel's smaller, he bosses Rudy around."

"That's a dachsie for you," said Professor Wagstaff. "A big dog in a little-dog body."

Maisie yipped, yelped and chuckled when she saw me. I gave her a good head butt hello, then thumped my forepaws on the ground: "Let's play!"

She thumped her forepaws in reply. The two of us ganged up on Rudy and chased him to the far fence and back.

Professor Wagstaff was laughing when we returned.

"The old girl's like a youngster again when she plays with you, Strudel," he said. "We'll have to come back soon."

Rudy and I started to take a second lap, but Maisie was panting so I slowed down.

"Strudel," she said when she'd caught her breath, "how have you been? Has your forever home been everything you hoped for?"

So much had happened. Where to begin? I had saved my family from mean, rotten varmints. I had protected them from bad guys and outlaws and villains. Just like Chief, I had prevailed over evil and made sure that peace and justice triumphed.

Not to brag or anything.

I started to tell her all that, then stopped. There would be more play dates and more chances to talk. For now, I cut to the chase.

"I followed your advice, Maisie. When things went

wrong, I reminded myself to live in the present, and I summoned my hound-dog nature. I could never have done it without you."

My modest old friend dipped her snout. I think she wanted to argue, but before she could, Jake called me over. "Strudel, c'mere! Professor Wagstaff brought you something. He says you especially like them. Is that right? I never knew."

I couldn't see what Jake had in his hand, but I could smell it—*butter cookie*!

Tragically, the treat was swallowed before I had the chance to fully taste it.

Meanwhile, Maisie laughed. "You've done a lot of growing up since I last saw you, Strudel. But in some ways, you haven't changed."

Thirty-Nine

It was full-on spring before I found out what had happened to Capo and Pepito. On most days the sun shone. The trees had budded out. The smellscape was fantastic. Out on the patio, Oscar, Johanna and I enjoyed many a pleasant chat.

On a Friday after school, Jake and I were on our way to the dog park when Mrs. Rodino turned the corner and came down the sidewalk toward us. She was walking with a dark-haired girl a few years younger than Jake. Both of them carried cat-sized plastic pet carriers.

"Hello, Jake!" Mrs. Rodino set her carrier down on the sidewalk. "Meet my granddaughter, Pamela. She and I are on our way back from the vet. Nothing serious, just vaccinations. Have a look at that stray you brought me. He's in the carrier here." She pointed with her toe. "Of course you remember?"

"Sure I do." Jake bent down and peeked through the carrier's wire door. "Oh my gosh—I can hardly believe it's the same cat!"

I jumped up and leaned my paws on Jake's shoulder so I could get a look. In the carrier was Pepito, but he had been transformed! Now he was a snowy-white feline so fluffy you could almost have called him beautiful . . . if it were possible for a feline to be beautiful. As for the putrid smell, it had been replaced with a different one, equally disgusting—shampoo.

"All Ichabod needed was decent food and a lot of washing up," Mrs. Rodino said.

"You named him Ichabod?" Jake asked.

"After a scrawny schoolteacher in an old story," said Mrs. Rodino.

"How is the other one doing?" Jake asked. "The shy fat one?"

"Here he is, I've got him," said Pamela. "He's just my biggest-wiggest-widdle *baby!*"

In her carrier was Capo, head resting on his forepaws, eyes narrowed to slits, obviously wishing he were anywhere else at that moment. Unlike Pepito, he looked physically the same as before. But his formerly arrogant expression was now humble, embarrassed even.

That wasn't the best part, though. The best part was his *clothes*—a cloth bonnet and a purple dress, which must have been made for a human baby.

"Isn't his outfit just the most adorable?" Pamela asked. "Grandma let me buy it at the thrift store. It's just so perfect for my fatty-watty!"

Jake looked at Pamela. "Is that his name—Fatty-Watty?"

Pamela giggled. "Don't be silly. No one would give a cat that name. *My* kitty is called Mr. Fuzzybum."

"Get me out of here!" Capo yowled.

"Are you kidding? You never had it so good!" I said. "Have a nice life, Capo . . . or should I say Mr. Fuzzybum?"

Mrs. Rodino lifted up the white cat's carrier. "We better get moving, but I do want to thank you again, Jake. Till these characters showed up, I didn't realize how lonely I was. They've been a project for sure. At first, the big guy did not want to be an indoor cat. But he's a good boy now. He even puts up with Pamela's special brand of affection."

After Mrs. Rodino and Pamela walked on, I surprised Jake with an outburst of sheer joy—tail-wagging, jumping, yipping and spinning.

"Strudel, sheesh!" Jake bent down to corral me and untangle my leash. "What's got into you?"

What's got into me? I'll tell you—I am happy-happy-happy!

Not only that, I couldn't wait to tell Oscar and Johanna how things had gone for the cruel and fearsome leader of the Pier 67 Gang. Not even Thesiger Sheed Lewis could have written a better ending for a villain.

That night Grandpa came over as usual with pizza, and the conversation turned to yours truly.

"For a wiener dog," Grandpa said, "Killer there's looking pretty handsome these days. You must be taking good care of him, Jake."

Jake said, "Thanks. I am."

I thumped my tail.

"The kid's quite the responsible dog owner," said Mom. "I'm proud of him for that. As for Strudel, even Laura likes him now."

Mutanski grunted. "Strudel's okay, I guess. Anyway, I'm stuck with him just like I'm stuck with everyone else in this family."

"Speaking of family . . ." Grandpa cleared his throat. "I, uh . . . have an announcement to make. Betty Rossi and I, well, we're planning on getting married."

I don't know much about this "married" thing, but I could tell what Grandpa said was important. Nobody said a word for several moments. Nobody even swallowed. Was there going to be snapping and snarling? I held my breath and waited.

Finally Mom broke the silence. "Dad," she said, a big smile in her voice, "that is wonderful news. Congratulations."

Grandpa said, "That's a relief. I wasn't sure how you'd react."

"Are we supposed to call Mrs. Rossi 'Grandma' now?" Jake asked.

"Up to you," Grandpa said.

"Sheesh," said Mutanski. "First a dog. Now a grandma? We're like a real family all of a sudden."

"Just like a real family," said Jake. "Can I have another slice of pizza?"

"Sure," said Mom. "There's enough for everyone."

The End